Other Scholastic books by Martyn Godfrey:

Alien Wargames
The Day the Sky Exploded
Here She Is, Ms Teeny-Wonderful
It Isn't Easy Being Ms Teeny-Wonderful
Send in Ms Teeny Wonderful
Wally Stutzgummer, Super Bad Dude
I Spent My Summer Vacation Kidnapped into Space
The Great Science Fair Disaster
There's a Cow in My Swimming Pool (with Frank O'Keeffe)
Monsters in the School
Meet You in the Sewer

Scholastic Canada Ltd
123 Newkirk Road, Richmond Hill, Ontario, Canada L4C 3G5

Scholastic Inc.
555 Broadway, New York, NY 10012, USA

Ashton Scholastic Limited
Private Bag 1, Penrose, Auckland, New Zealand

Ashton Scholastic Pty Limited
PO Box 579, Gosford, NSW 2250, Australia

Scholastic Publications Ltd.
Villiers House, Clarendon Avenue, Leamington Spa
Warwickshire, CV32 5PR, UK

Canadian Cataloguing in Publication Data

Godfrey, Martyn
Just call me Boom Boom

(JAWS mob series ; 2)
ISBN 0-590-73081-9

I. Title. II. Series: Godfrey, Martyn. JAWS mob ; 2.

PS8563.08165J8 1994 jC813'.54 C93-095323-1
PZ7.G63Ju 1994

6 5 4 3 2 1 Printed in Canada 4 5 6 7 8/9

The J.A.W.S Mob

MARTYN GODFREY

Just call me BOOM BOOM

The J·A·W·S Mob

MARTYN GODFREY

Just call me BOOM BOOM

Cover by

SHARIF TARABAY

Scholastic Canada Ltd.

To Carolyn — who should have had her name here a long time ago.

Contents

The JAWS Mob is a writing club that meets informally at lunch time and after three-thirty in John Allen Watson School, a middle school in Toronto's West York neighborhood. Except for a few minor suggestions by myself on style and content, these are the original words of the JAWS Mob students. *Just Call Me Boom Boom* was written by an eighth grader, Bryan Bortorowski.

Ms Patricia Chang
Teacher Advisor
JAWS Mob

Chapter 1

Boom Boom

The line-up in the JAWS cafeteria was longer than usual. The heat was something fierce. I felt a red claw gripping my gut, tighter and tighter. I was on the verge of losing my temper. In a minute, somebody was going to be sorry.

Very sorry.

My buddy, Soso Hayes, was in front of me. Behind me was a sixth grader with a dopey haircut. The line pushed forward and the kid rammed his empty tray into my back. I twisted around and glared at him, showing him my best snarl.

His eyes opened wide as he tried to take a step backward.

"I'm real sorry," he said sheepishly. "It wasn't my fault. I was pushed."

"You trying to get me mad?" I growled. "If you want to get me mad, then shove your stupid tray into my back again. Then I'll take your stupid tray and break it over your head. Understand?"

The little guy gulped and nodded. "Yes, sir."

"Take it easy, Boom Boom," Soso said. "You'll give the kid a heart attack. Look at him. He thinks you're the Incredible Hulk." Then Soso leaned around me so he could speak to the sixth grader.

"Don't worry about it, little comrade. Boom Boom's not going to break anything over anybody's head. He just acts the mean machine. He's really a nice guy." Then Soso whispered into my ear, "Remember your promise to Mrs. Bush."

I took a long deep breath to help me cool down. Then I shouted to the front of the line, "We haven't got all day! We're going to die of starvation back here."

Why was it so hot? What was taking so long?

"So what do you say?" Soso spoke softly. "Would you like to explore the Watson Mansion with me?"

"'Course I would. But everybody knows you can't get into that old place. It's fenced off and boarded up."

"I know a way," Soso bragged. "Meet me by The Bridge tonight at seven. I'll bring a couple of flashlights."

"I can't tonight," I told him. "I've got something to do."

"What?" Soso wondered.

"Just something. It's none of your business. It's personal and private."

Soso seemed surprised by my surly answer. "That's cool, BB Man. I don't need to know if you don't want me to know."

And I didn't want him to know, either. I didn't want anybody in JAWS to know. If anybody at school found out what I was going to do that evening, I'd get laughed out of the neighborhood. It would be so bad that I'd have to move.

The line surged again and the sixth grader jabbed his tray into my back a second time.

"That's it!" I yelled. "I'm going to — "

"Think, Boom Boom," Soso reminded me quickly. "Mrs. Bush. You promised her. Think of what'll happen if you break your promise."

I swiveled around and grunted at the kid, low and fierce, like I was some kind of giant bear. I immediately regretted it.

The expression on the kid's face was one of genuine fear. I'd terrified the little guy. I hadn't meant to do that. I was just getting so mad waiting in the hot cafeteria line, I had to get angry at something.

"I'm really, really sorry," the sixth grader said pleadingly. "It wasn't my fault. Honest."

"That's okay," I grumbled. "Just don't do it again."

"Okay, I won't. Thanks, Mr. Boom Boom."

I was a little surprised that he knew my nickname. It seemed that everybody in school was calling me Boom Boom nowadays. Even people I didn't know. My real name is Bryan Benjamin Bortorowski, but I've been called Boom Boom ever since kindergarten. I've always been the biggest kid in my class. When I was younger, I used to get into fights with the older kids. Not often, two or three times a week at most, but enough that my kindergarten teacher said, "You sure are a loose cannon. Boom. Boom. Boom."

The name stuck. As if he was reading my mind, Soso said, "You know, you don't really deserve your nickname any more. I mean, you're still the biggest kid in the school, but it just struck me that you went through all of seventh grade last year without getting into a single fight with an eighth grader."

"It wasn't easy," I replied. "There was a truckload of people who deserved a bonk on the head."

"And now we're the oldest kids in the school," Soso concluded. "So there's nobody older left for you to fight. Maybe we should start calling you Bryan."

"Stick with Boom Boom," I insisted. Then I called to the kids at the front of the line, "I'm getting gray hair back here. Get your food and move it!"

As if on command, the line began to shuffle forward. Soso helped himself to a salad from the cooler. "You want one, Boom Boom?"

"No. Why is it so hot in here? How come JAWS doesn't have air conditioning?" I took a juice box off the shelf, shoved in the straw and took a long swallow. This cold apple juice will help, I thought. It's going to be okay. I'm under control. I'm going to be fine.

Wrong.

The line suddenly stopped. Soso took a step backward and stomped on my foot. Stomp is the right word. The heel of his Nike massacred my toes.

"Yeow!" I yelled as pain flowered in my brain.

The red claw of anger surged through my intestines, flew up my arms, and exploded in my head. I was indignant. Furious. How could Soso dare to step on my foot?

I turned the juice box upside down and squeezed the contents over Soso's salad.

"Hey, man," he protested. "What did you do that for?"

"Boom Boom!"

I recognized the voice of Mr. Ahnassey, my Homeroom and Core teacher. He was obviously on cafeteria supervision.

"I think you'd better take a walk to the office and have a talk with Mrs. Bush."

Five minutes later, I was standing in the assistant principal's office.

"I'm extremely disappointed, Bryan," Mrs. Bush lectured.

She was using my regular name instead of calling me Boom Boom. That meant she was really upset. She grabbed a Kleenex from the box on her desk and used it to attack the lenses of her glasses. Then she shoved the glasses onto her nose and stared up at me. The lenses magnified her eyes, and I had no trouble picturing her as a demented owl.

"Extremely disappointed," she repeated. "You're in eighth grade now. Why do you insist on acting like a little baby?"

I blew out my breath between my teeth, slow and forceful, and tried to relax the muscles tightening the back of my neck and shoulders. "Cool it," I said to myself. "Stay calm. It'll all be over in a few minutes. Don't say nothing."

I shifted my weight from one foot to the other and studied her office, hoping I could distract myself.

Mrs. Bush's office doesn't seem to change between my frequent visits, I thought. The same books are always on the shelf. The same diplomas hang on the wall. It always seems that the same mess of papers covers the top of her desk.

"I hate starting the week this way," Mrs. Bush complained. She ripped a piece off the Kleenex. "It's only Monday and I already wish it was Friday. Do you remember the promise you made to me after you threw Vanessa's binder out of the science room window on Friday, Bryan?"

"Of course I do," I answered.

"You promised that you'd start the week with a new attitude. You told me that I'd see a different Bryan today, one who knows how to control his temper."

I tried to speak calmly, but my voice came out ragged around the edges. "I got mad because Soso stepped on my foot in the cafeteria line. Surely I'm allowed to get a little ticked about that, aren't I, Mrs. B.?"

Mrs. Bush sighed. "You're allowed to be miffed."

"Miffed?"

"Mildly disturbed by the circumstances," Mrs. Bush explained.

"Okay," I agreed. "I was miffed a whole lot. I'm sorry."

She sighed again. "It's getting to the point where being sorry is not good enough. Soso didn't step on your foot on purpose. Squeezing the contents of your juice box over his lunch was definitely an overreaction."

"Give me a break, Mrs. Bush," I pleaded. "Maybe chucking Vanessa's binder out the window last week wasn't exactly right. But, like I told you on Friday, she laughed at me when Mrs. Murtz caught me sleeping in Science. Give me credit. My first thought was to throw Vanessa out the window, but I didn't. Not that I ever would, of course. But the thought did pass through my head. So I did control my temper, sort of.

"And today, my first thought was to dump the juice over Soso's head. I didn't do that because Soso is my buddy and I'd never want to embarrass him. So I didn't really lose my temper in the cafeteria either, when you look at it that way."

"That's just nonsense," she declared. "Your childish tantrums have been a constant nuisance to me ever since you started JAWS in sixth grade. I thought things would be different this year. You're in eighth grade after all. But I was wrong. It's not even Halloween and you've already been in my office six times."

"Only for minor things," I defended.

She arched her eyebrows and tore the last few pieces of tissue. They rested in a sorry pile on her messy desk.

"Minor? Do you consider trashing your locker door a minor thing?"

"I didn't trash it," I said. "I put a dent in the bottom when I kicked it because Mr. Horvath had just cut me from the school soccer team. It was a cheap door. I paid for the repairs. Besides, I won't do anything like that again. I realize it was immature."

The assistant principal rolled on. "If you don't start treating your fellow students and school property with respect, I will revoke all your privileges. That means no school dances. No field trips. No Scavenger Hunt Team. And no JAWS Mob."

"No JAWS Mob!" I gasped. "But I need the writing club, Mrs. B. Writing stuff helps me keep my cool."

"Well, it doesn't appear to be helping very much, does it?" she said sarcastically.

For a moment, I felt the bubbling redness rising

up from the bottom of my guts. Why didn't Mrs. Bush know I was keeping my promise as best as I could?

"Do you understand the consequences of any future incidents, Bryan? Something like this must not happen again."

"Yes, Mrs. Bush," I said through my teeth.

She nodded her head. "Good. The first thing thing you can do is apologize to Soso. He's waiting outside."

"Yes, Mrs. Bush."

"Boom Boom," she said as I opened the door. "You are a good student. Your report cards are consistently excellent. The teachers tell me that they enjoy having you in their classes. And despite your frequent hot-headed outbursts, you are popular with your fellow students. If only you can learn to control yourself, you will be an exceptional young man."

"Yes, Mrs. Bush."

• • •

Soso Hayes was leaning on the counter, sprucing his hair with a pick. He looked miffed. "Finally," he grumbled. "You go bananas in the cafeteria and *I* get punished. Why did Mrs. Bush make me wait here until you came out?"

"You're waiting so I can apologize to you," I told him. "I'm sorry."

"It's cool, Boom Boom Man."

"I really am sorry," I told him. "I like your new haircut. It looks okay all flat on top."

"A compliment? To what do I owe this?"

"I guess I feel stupid about the juice. I was just frustrated because Mrs. Bush picks on me."

"Like I said, it's cool. See you later, mon frère. Remember the Watson Mansion tomorrow. The Bridge at seven. We'll go ghost hunting."

Chapter 2

JAWS Mob

After school, I beelined straight to the computer room for JAWS Mob. Ms Chang, the computer teacher, smiled at me as I walked through the door.

"Right on time, Boom Boom," she said. "As always."

I smiled at her and wished she'd think of some other way to say hello to me every night after school. Ms Chang had a lot of annoying little habits which got under my skin. But I tried not to say anything. I always tried extra hard to be polite to her, and most of the time I succeeded. I worried that if Ms Chang ever found a reason to kick me out of JAWS Mob, I'd be terminally miserable.

Sitting next to Ms Chang was a guy about her age. He wasn't a JAWS teacher and I didn't recognize him as one of the subs. Ms Chang must have noticed the puzzled expression on my face because she introduced me.

"Boom Boom, I'd like you to meet Raymond Trout. Mr. Trout is a friend of mine."

They looked at each other and immediately broke into silly grins. I quickly deduced that they were close friends.

"Mr. Trout is here to fix the broken Mac," Ms Chang told me. "He works with computers."

"That's nice." I was anxious to sit down and get on with my story.

"I'm glad to meet you," Mr. Trout said. "Ms Chang has mentioned you several times."

I wondered what that meant.

"I work at Wonder World," Mr. Trout announced.

That got my attention. "You work on the rides?"

He nodded. "I guess you could say that. I operate the computer that runs the whole park. Everything is run by computer, you know. The roller coaster has to be going exactly the right speed through those triple loops."

"Why? Would the cars fall off if it was going too slow?" I asked.

"No, but it would be an uncomfortable ride. We're more concerned with the rides going too quickly. I take it you've been to Wonder World?"

"Lots of times."

"Then you know the Weird Water ride?"

"One of my favorites."

"If that ride goes even ten percent faster than it's supposed to, the little car will smash to pieces when it hits the water pond."

"Wow," I said. "Your job must be really hard."

"Actually, it's pretty easy. The computer is just like you have at school. All the commands are stored on a hard drive and . . . " He reached into his sports jacket pocket and held up a floppy disk. " . . . this is my security disk which lets me access the hard drive."

"Awesome. You mean, if I had that disk I'd be able to mess around with the rides at Wonder World?"

Raymond Trout shook his head. "Not quite. You'd have to know my secret code word first."

"You must have one of the best jobs in the world."

"It's a little boring sometimes," he confessed. "But speaking of which, I have to get to work now." He turned to Ms Chang. "I'll see you tomorrow, Pat."

I had the distinct impression that, if they were alone, they would be kissing at this point.

"I better get to work too," I said to excuse myself.

I marched to a computer and sat down. I noticed Ms Chang's boyfriend leave at the same time that a friend of mine, JB Lunn, entered the room. JB picked his disk up off Ms Chang's desk and went to his computer.

I got back into my latest story. It was called "Giggling Girls From Outer Space," and I hoped to enter it in the humorous category in the JAWS writing contest the following month.

"You want me to what?" Jason wondered.

"We want you to come back and live on our planet with us," the tall, cute girl with the antennae explained.

"Why would I want to do that?" Jason went on. "I like it here on Earth."

"Our planet is much better than Earth," the shorter, equally cute girl with no eyelids giggled. "Besides, on our world you'd be the only boy."

"The only boy?" Jason gasped. "What happened to all the others?"

"We've never had any boys on our world," they giggled together. "But we'd really like one."

Jason shook his head. "I don't know. What would I do?"

They blushed and continued to giggle.

"Can I think about it?"

"Of course," they said as they headed back to their flying saucer, giggling to each other. "Think of all the fun things you could do being the only boy on a planet inhabited by five billion giggling girls. We'll be back after supper. You can tell us your decision then."

"That's an interesting fantasy you have," Ms

Chang announced. She was standing behind me, reading my monitor. Sneaking up behind me rates on the top of my list of Ms Chang's annoying habits. She does it all the time, and it drives me nuts. But once again, I didn't say anything.

"A fantasy? It's not my fantasy, Ms Chang. It's just a humorous story. I'm going to — "

She didn't let me finish. "No need to be embarrassed," she whispered. "I remember what it was like being your age. I used to have my little fantasies too."

The way she jumps to the wrong conclusions a lot of the time annoys me something fierce.

I was about to mention this fact, but fortunately, Vanessa Rodriguez, who was sitting on the other side of the room, called out, "Is it okay if I use the modem, Ms Chang? I want to send my story to my penpal in St. Albert."

"Certainly," the teacher answered. "That's why we have it."

I watched Vanessa glide over to the computer attached to the modem.

I still have a soft spot for Vanessa. I don't think anybody would argue with the fact that she's extremely good-looking.

Last June, I asked her if she'd like to go out with me. She didn't want to. But she didn't really shoot me down in flames. She was very polite about it. "I'm sorry, Boom Boom," she'd told me. "It's not that I don't like you. It's just that I like JB a whole lot more."

But ever since I saw the newspaper girl, I'd stopped thinking about Vanessa.

Ms Chang raised her voice and spoke to the entire room. "I have to go to the library for a few minutes, everyone. I expect perfect behavior, as usual."

I glanced around the room. My fellow JAWS Mob members were busy plunking away on their keyboards. That is, all except one. I noticed JB Lunn peering at his screen with a bewildered look on his face.

Which immediately struck me as weird.

I knew JB was working on a story about his adventure in the West York Community Hall a couple of weeks ago. Why would he look so confused? I stood up and walked over.

"What's up, JB?" I asked as I slid into the chair next to him. "You got a problem with your story?"

JB shook his head. "I made a mistake. I left my disk on Ms Chang's desk at lunch time. When I came in a minute ago I thought I was picking it up, but I got the wrong disk."

I studied the screen. There was a silver, star-shaped symbol at the top of the monitor. I recognized it as the same one that shone atop the main gates of Wonder World. It was the Wonder World logo. Underneath the star was written `Welcome to Wonder World. Please enter your security code to gain access.`

"Weird, huh?" JB said.

"Mega-weird," I agreed. "Pop the disk."

JB did as I asked. I pulled it out of the drive and read the label out loud. "This disk is the property of Wonder World and is intended for use by authorized Wonder World personnel only. Any attempt to use this disk by persons other than those designated by Wonder World is a criminal offense punishable by law."

On the other side was a paste-on label. Written on it in pen was, "Raymond Trout, Wonder World Computer Technician. Tenderlo . . . " The Tenderlo was all smudged. There may have been more letters once upon a time, but they were now just an ink smudge.

"Holy," I said. "This belongs to Ms Chang's boyfriend. That guy who was leaving as you were coming in. He must have put it on her desk and forgotten it."

"You think Ms Chang will dump on me for using it?" JB wondered.

"She's not here. Even if she was, it's not your fault this Raymond Trout left it, is it? Fire the disk back in."

"I don't know, Boom Boom. All that fancy talk on the label means it's against the law to use this disk," JB pointed out.

"They're just empty words. They have to do that. It's to stop people from copying and stuff. It doesn't mean nothing. It's like the warning they stick at the beginning of movie videos. Nobody pays any attention. Besides, that Trout guy told me it was just a security disk to get access to the hard drive of the Wonder World computer. Since we don't have the Wonder World computer, we can't do anything wrong, can we?"

"I'll take your word for it," JB rationalized as he took the disk from me and slipped it back into the drive. "I just hope Ms Chang doesn't find out."

"We're not going to do anything wrong," I repeated. "I'm curious. Let's see what happens."

He nodded. "Okay."

Welcome to Wonder World. Please enter your security code to gain access reappeared on the screen.

"Type in Ms Chang's boyfriend's name," I instructed.

JB entered Raymond Trout.

Invalid code, the screen read. Access denied.

"If it's not his own name, then maybe it's his wife's name," I said. "I read in *Hacker* magazine that most code words are something easy, something personal to the person who uses it."

"How could Raymond Trout be going out with Ms Chang if he's married?" JB wondered.

"Oh, right," I said. "Maybe it's his girlfriend's name. Type in Patricia Chang."

Invalid code. Access denied.

"Maybe it's the name of one of his old girlfriends. Start typing some girls' names."

"Like who?"

"Girls we know. Girls in our class. Girls we know in the school."

He typed `Rupinder.`

`Invalid code. Access denied.`

`Vanessa.`

`Invalid code. Access denied.`

`Erin.`

`Invalid code. Access denied.`

Thirty names later, we were getting frustrated.

"Maybe he's got a nephew. Start with the names of guys we know," I suggested.

JB typed `Bryan.`

`Invalid code. Access denied.`

He keyed `Malweet.`

`Invalid code. Access denied.`

`Roberto.`

`Invalid Code. Access denied.`

The same message after every name.

Finally, JB typed `Boom Boom.`

`Invalid Code. Access denied.`

"Try your name," I suggested.

"No way," he said with a chuckle. "It might be recording this. I don't want the cops after me."

"Why would the police be after you?" Ms Chang asked. She'd obviously finished her work in the library and was parked behind us.

What is it with her? flashed through my mind. *She's worse than a ninja, always creeping up behind people.*

"What is that?" The teacher pointed at JB's monitor. "What program is this?"

"We're not sure, Ms Chang," JB explained, ejecting the Wonder World disk.

She ordered him to hand it to her. As she examined the label, anger lines etched her face. "Do you boys know what this warning says?"

I looked at JB. He glanced at me.

"Well?" Ms Chang asked. "Do you know what's written on the label?"

"Kind of," JB stuttered.

"Yeah, we know, Ms Chang," I announced. "But it's no big deal. Your boyfriend must have left it. We weren't doing anything wrong. We were just messing around."

The anger creases got a little sharper. "I am extremely disappointed in both of you. The warning on this label is in plain English. You can understand what it says. You are not allowed to mess around with this disk."

"We're sorry," JB said.

"Sorry?" Ms Chang went on in her angry teacher voice. "Not only are you breaking the law, you are also breaking my trust. I trust you to respect the rules of the computer room."

The way Ms Chang doesn't listen to explanations

gets under my skin. I was trying to be polite, but I was losing it fast. First, Mrs. Bush at lunch. Now Ms Chang after school. I only had so much patience.

"What rules?" I pointed at the Classroom Rules poster pinned to the bulletin board. They covered how to treat the hardware and software with respect, how not to hog the computer, stuff like that. There was nothing about messing with any disks we found. "Where does it say we're not allowed to experiment?"

Ms Chang reared back. I pictured flames shooting out her eyes. "Boom Boom! Do not talk to me that way!"

"But it's no big deal, Ms C.," I repeated. "What harm did we do? If you want my advice, Ms Chang, I think you should relax a bit. Getting upset about something like this isn't good for your blood pressure."

I knew I was being rude, and in the back of my head, I knew I could be jeopardizing my status as a JAWS Mob member, but the bubbling redness was sending little fizzes into my head.

Ms Chang opened her mouth, then quickly shut it, biting her bottom lip. I'd seen a few teachers do that in my day. I knew she wanted to say something to me that teachers aren't supposed to say to their students.

At the same time I was being rude, I was also feeling a little proud of myself. The old me would have said something like, "That's better, Ms Chang.

You'll live longer if you learn how to chill out." I figured what I did say was a definite improvement.

So, being a rational and mature human being, I said, "I guess now would be a good time for me to go home, huh?"

She still didn't say anything. She just nodded, biting her lip so hard it was as white as her teeth.

"See you, JB," I said as I went back to my computer and retrieved my disk.

"Boom Boom," Ms Chang called.

I turned around and noticed everyone else in computer club looking at me.

"What you did with Raymond's disk was wrong," Ms Chang said slowly. "If anything like this ever happens again, you'll be in the deepest trouble possible."

S. Storoni
WSPA
World Society for the Protection of Animals

Chapter 3

The Newspaper Girl

I left JAWS and began walking home down Watson Street. A dozen steps outside the school yard, Erin Anderson, a sixth grader, jogged up beside me. She was lugging a heavy-looking book. "Hey, Boom Boom," she said. "Walk home with you?"

"If you want, but I'm in a pretty rotten mood," I told her. "This hasn't been one of my better days."

"I notice you have a lot of those, huh?" she said. "But I know how to cure that. Let's play Animal."

"Get serious, Erin," I grumped. "For the hundredth time, I don't want to play a game where I have to act like a stupid animal so you can guess what I am. I'm in eighth grade, not kindergarten."

She stared up at me, her wild green eyes gleaming under her bushy eyebrows. "You eighth graders think you're all grown up. You're not. You should try playing Animal. I think you'd like it. There's a couple of animals you could do real good."

"Is that some kind of insult?" I asked. "Are you going to tell me that I'd be a good gorilla or something?"

"Heck, no," Erin answered. "I was thinking you'd be a great Ring-Eyed Wombat because of your big brown eyes. Or even a White-Tufted Lemur because of your tiny nose."

I just shook my head. "You sure are strange. You sure they didn't kick you out of Alberta?"

She chuckled. "Don't tell anyone, okay? I don't want to get kicked out of Toronto, too. I'm just starting to like it here."

Erin had only started at JAWS a couple of weeks before, after moving from Lethbridge. But I knew her pretty well already because JB spends a lot of time with her. JB's dad and Erin's mom have started dating, and Erin helped JB during his Community Hall adventure.

Although I haven't told Erin, I feel the same way about her as I feel about my younger sister. I feel like I should protect her. Erin's spacey and weird, but it's a cute weirdness. I respect people who are a little different. Trouble is, a lot of other people don't. Kids like Erin tend to get picked on. But if anyone picks on Erin, they have to answer to me.

"You seen JB?" Erin asked.

"Yeah, he's still in the computer room. He and I just got heck from Ms Chang. That's why I'm in a rotten mood." I told her about the Wonder World disk.

"I can see Ms Chang's point," she announced when I finished. "Then again, it's not like you were going to do anything. Maybe you both over-reacted."

I pointed at the book she was carrying. "What's that about? It looks old."

"It is," she told me. "It was printed way back in 1949. We're studying Toronto's history in Social Studies. This book is called *Famous Families of Toronto*. It's about the people who founded the city. You know, the Eatons, the Phillips, people like that."

"Sounds boring."

"It isn't. It's kind of like an old *People* magazine. It tells the interesting stuff about the families. There's a chapter on the Watson family. Did you know that John Allen Watson was shipwrecked when he sailed here from England in 1839? If he hadn't been rescued we wouldn't have a school today. I mean, we'd have it, but it would be called something different."

"Fascinating."

"Hey, Boom Boom, do you like the girl who delivers the *West Yorker*?"

I was so stunned by her comment that I stopped walking. "What . . . why would you think that?"

Erin stopped too, peering at me from under her thick eyebrows. "Because I saw you following her through the park last Monday."

"You saw me?"

She nodded. "Sure did. You were spying on her in the park, hiding behind the bushes and garbage cans. So I spied on you."

"You spied on me?"

"Yeah. You looked pretty mysterious. I wondered what you were doing."

"You spied on me?" I growled.

"What are you getting mad about?" she queried. "You were spying on her. It's the same thing."

I couldn't argue with that. The gravity of what she'd just said struck me. She'd seen me following a girl and spying on her like a weirdo. If this got out, my reputation would be shot. I'd be the laughing stock of JAWS. Of the whole neighborhood. Even if people didn't laugh in my face, they'd sure do a lot of laughing behind my back.

Erin was talking about a girl I had first seen two weeks before. She delivers the community newspaper, the *West Yorker*, which comes out every Monday. I was watching TV when I saw her through the living room window. She tromped up my front steps and slam-dunked a *West Yorker* into my mailbox. She had to be from West York School because I'd never noticed her around JAWS.

I guess the first thing that attracted me to her was her size. She's almost as big as I am. There aren't many thirteen-year-old girls who can claim that. But add to that her long frizzy hair and round expressive face, and you have the world's most attractive girl.

I saw her again in Yeung's Variety Store the next day, searching through the ice cream freezer. She looked so cute, all bent over, ripping open the various boxes until she found the Fudgsicles. It would have been so easy for me to walk up to her and introduce myself. I could've trotted over and said, "I like Fudgsicles too. Do you want to rip open a box for me, please?"

The only problem was, I couldn't. For some stupid reason, I hid behind the cereal and PopTarts and stared at her. That's right, me, Boom Boom Bortorowski, the toughest kid in JAWS, stared at her from a hiding place.

Of course, I felt super ashamed of myself for being such a jerk. I went home and drove my fist through my pillow. A few hundred times. When I was finished, there were foam chips all over my room.

"I'll buy a new one," I'd told my mom. "Maybe you should complain to the store. They should sew pillow cases better."

That was two weeks ago. Last week, I acted even more stupid.

On Monday, I hid in the shrubs outside my house so I could get a closer look at the newspaper girl. After she'd finished delivering the *West Yorker* to my street, I followed her through Watson Park. That must have been when Erin saw me.

"You saw me?" I said again.

"You like her, huh?" Erin probed. "You're just too shy to talk to her, right?"

I put on my best angry face. "You tell anybody and I'll . . . "

Erin waved her hand in the air. "I'm your friend. I'm not going to tell anybody. Except JB, of course. I've already told him. I tell him everything because I've got the strong feeling his dad and my mom will get married some day. Then he and I will be brother and sister."

I let out my breath in an angry *snnaarrllffkk.*

"You don't have to get mad. I'm not going to reveal your secret, Boom Boom. Look, if it makes you feel any better, I'll tell you a secret about myself that I haven't told anybody."

"What's that got to do with anything?"

"A lot. If you know something about me that I don't want anybody to know, it means I won't tell about you spying on the newspaper girl. I'll tell you a special secret. When I was two and a half, I used to pee down the heating vents," Erin said.

"What?"

"I used to pee down the vents in the floor," she repeated. "I don't know why I did it. I was just a dumb little kid and I'm not proud of it now."

"That's gross."

She shook her head. "No, gross is what happened when the furnace came on. You should have smelled the house."

"I'm glad I didn't."

"If I ever tell anybody about you spying on the *West Yorker* girl, you can tell people about me and the heating vents, okay? Feel any better?"

I nodded. After her confession, I knew I could trust Erin, but I didn't feel completely better. I was still pretty angry at myself for being caught spying. Or maybe I was angry at what I was about to do.

Again.

"So now you feel better," Erin said enthusiastically. "Let's play Animal."

I glanced at my watch. "I can't. I got something important to do."

"Bet I know what it is," she said.

"See you later," I said as I trotted away.

I rushed home, dumped my books, and sat on my front step. Trying to appear super casual, I checked up and down the street to see if Erin had followed me. She hadn't. Maybe she did know what I was going to do, but if she didn't see it, she couldn't prove it.

Five minutes later, I saw the object of my admiration, the *West Yorker* girl, turn the corner. I dove behind the honeysuckle bushes and positioned myself so I could study her without being seen.

After a few moments, she was strolling up my walk. Why do you want to talk to her so bad? I wondered. What is it about the way she kind of half-steps, half-stomps as she walks that makes you want to get to know her so bad?

When the girl got to the top step, she dropped the newspaper into the mailbox. Then she leaned over the railing and cupped her hand over her eyes so she could peer through the living room window. She surveyed the interior of the house for a good ten seconds.

Odd, I thought. What's that all about? As she thudded down the steps, she studied the honeysuckle bushes for a moment. My heart pounded. What if she could see me? But she started whistling as she skip-thumped down the walk. As soon as she crossed the street, I charged from the bushes and raced down the road to the park. I headed straight for The Bridge.

The Bridge is a covered bridge built over York Creek a long time ago by John Allen Watson when the creek was still part of his farm. The city has kept it in good repair. It's a local attraction. I've even seen tourists taking pictures of it.

I ran along the jogging path and into The Bridge. There are lot of fancy cut-out windows in The Bridge's wall. I hoisted my foot into one of them and boosted myself up into the rafters. I squatted tightrope-style on a beam, resting one hand on the inside of the roof for support. I smiled in anticipation. The *West Yorker* girl would be along any minute now.

"What you doing, Boom Boom?" a voice asked.

Two little girls were staring up at me. I recognized one of them as Janice Lunn, JB's sister. "What does it look like? I'm playing Animal. I'm pretending I'm a bat. Get lost."

"Can we play?" Janice wanted to know.

"What are you? Deaf? Take a hike. And take your bimbo friend with you."

"This is Carrie Anderson," Janice went on. "She's not a bimbo. She just moved into The Tower a few weeks ago. Maybe you know her sister, Erin?"

"Yeah, I know Erin. Beat it. Both of you. Get lost. Fade away. Amscray!"

"You want us to go, Boom Boom?"

"What was your first clue, Twit Twins?" Little kids can be extra thick sometimes.

Janice tugged on Carrie's sweatshirt. "We'd better go."

"He sure is rude," Carrie said as they left The Bridge.

"My brother says that Boom Boom invents new swear words all the time." Janice's voice trailed down the path.

I made a mental note to eat JB's binder to show him that I don't like comments made about me behind my back.

"Ooops!" I said out loud. I'd almost toppled off. My legs were cramping from balancing on the beam. Why hadn't the newspaper girl arrived yet? I wouldn't be able to stay up here much longer.

Another minute passed.

Suddenly, Soso pedaled through The Bridge on

his BMX. I resisted the urge to shout to him.

Another long minute.

Finally, I heard the *thump, thump* of sneakers. The top of a frizzy, long-haired head came into view. At the same moment, to my complete disbelief, my leg muscles cramped and I toppled off the beam.

I became a diving Icarus, and just like the stupid guy with the wax wings who flew too close to the sun, I became a mess of flailing arms and waving legs. Down. Down.

I landed with a solid *thadump* at the newspaper girl's feet.

"What the — " she shouted.

Chapter 4

Gusty

"Oh. Oooh," I groaned as I rolled over onto my back. I sucked short, shallow breaths and stared at the massive figure blocking the late afternoon sunlight.

The *West Yorker* girl was a blurry shape in my vision. She loomed over me, hands on her hips, newspaper bag swaying slightly off her left shoulder. Slowly, she sharpened into focus.

"You hurt?" she asked.

It was the voice of an angel. Her words weren't a question. They were a demand. Strong and tough, a touch of Klingon in her throat. What power. I'd never heard a girl who sounded like me before.

"You sure hit the ground hard," she said. "But none of your arms or legs are bent at a funny angle, so I guess you didn't bust anything. How do you feel?"

Cautiously, I propped myself up on my elbows and concentrated on my pain. My elbow hurt, but it was only scratched. And my hip throbbed — for sure I'd have a decent bruise for a few days. But nothing hurt real bad.

"I'm okay," I told her. "Everything's cool."

"Good," she said. "I want you to understand that I wouldn't even think of doing this if you were really hurt."

She reached into the paper bag, removed a *West Yorker*, carefully folded it into a tight roll, wound back like a clean-up batter going for a home-run fast ball, and took a swing at me.

She was aiming for my shoulder, but my reflexes made me pull away. Instinctively I bent over, trying to duck. The paper smacked me solidly on the side of the head.

KER-Thwack!

"Yeow!"

I've only seen stars twice in my life. The first time was in fourth grade. We were playing softball in the park when a group of eighth graders arrived and tried to take over the diamond. 'Course, I wasn't going to let them do that. So I picked out their leader and told him I'd shove my baseball bat through his ears if he didn't leave immediately. After he stopped laughing, he whomped me over the head with his catcher's mitt. Tiny lights had danced in my head for a full half-minute.

The second time was when the *West Yorker* girl thadunked me with our community newspaper. The stars were bigger this time, like freestyling magnesium flares. They whirled and spun in a kaleidoscope of colors. If my head hadn't stung so much, I might have found the swirling patterns interesting.

I rubbed my temple, waiting for the mini-galaxies to burn out. Then, when I was sure of my balance and that she wasn't going to hit me again, I stood up.

"What did you do that for?" I snarled. "There was no reason to hit me."

"I didn't mean to hit you on the head. I was aiming at your arm. You were stupid to duck," she snarled back. "And I hit you because you scared me, Maggot Nose! Nobody scares me unless they're looking for major trouble."

"Yeah, well, nobody hits me unless they're looking for a face full of bruises," I yelled. "If you weren't a girl you'd be weeping on the ground right now."

"Oh, yeah? Really? That's funny, but I don't believe you." She dropped the bag of papers and waved her fists in the air. "I think you're just mouthing off. I think those are just brave words, Bozo. I don't think you've got the guts to back them up. You think you can take me? How about you try it, right now?"

For a moment, the redness sped up through my body. I could feel the rage building. I was getting so fired, I'd soon be able to pound the Rice Krispies out of a runaway elephant. She wouldn't stand a chance. She'd be like a mosquito trapped in a can of Raid.

Then I realized what I was doing. As Soso had pointed out earlier, I hadn't been in a fight in over a year. I'd quit fighting because I knew it wasn't fair. I had the advantage because I was two sizes bigger than the guys who peeved me off. There's a big difference between being the meanest dude in the neighborhood and being a bully. There's no pride in shoving someone around just because you can. So I didn't do it.

And, even though at times, such as now, a girl might really deserve it, I would never hit a girl. Especially this girl.

So I concentrated on extinguishing the billowing redness in my head. I forced it to fade to crimson, then to ruby, then to rose, finally to pink. When I felt under control, I said. "I can't fight with you. I was mad enough to, but it's not my style. I don't want anybody to say Boom Boom Bortorowski has no class."

"Huh? Boom Boom Bortorowski?" She dropped her fists and looked suddenly impressed. "No kidding? Are you *the* Boom Boom Bortorowski?"

I nodded. "I'm the only one I know. Have you heard of me?"

"Who hasn't heard of Boom Boom Bortorowski? I should have figured it was you," she said. "I was fooled because somebody told me you looked big and stupid."

"Stupid?"

"That's why I was fooled. You're big — that's true. But you don't look stupid at all. You look terminally rude. That's a compliment."

"Thanks, I guess. But who is the turnip who said I look stupid?" I demanded.

"I can't tell you that, can I? You'd go look for him and I'd be aiding in a massacre.

She paused. "Wow, just think. Boom Boom Bortorowski. You're a legend at my school. Everybody knows you're the toughest kid at JAWS. When I noticed your house was on my paper route, I hoped I'd get a chance to meet you."

So that's what she was doing looking through my window, I thought.

"I hear even the high-schoolers don't mess with you. I'm pleased to meet you, Boom Boom. My name is Gusty Phipps."

"Gusty?"

She seemed to grow a size larger. "What's the matter? You don't like my name? Nobody teases me about my name unless they want a free nose job."

"I like it," I told her. "I like it a lot. It really suits you."

"It's short for Gustavia. My mother read the name in a romance novel before I was born."

"I said I like it."

"Good."

She pointed at the rafters. "So what were you doing up in the roof?"

I couldn't tell her I'd been spying on her. "Oh, I was just checking it out. Roofs are sort of a hobby of mine. You ever stop to take a close look at a roof? They're really fascinating. All that wood and metal and funny angles. Do you ever think about how useless buildings would be if they didn't have a roof? I believe that roofs are the most important invention in human history."

I expected her to tell me what an idiot I was. She didn't. "Never thought about it. I guess you're right, in a way. Look, Boom Boom, I'm sorry I hit you. I didn't mean to hurt you."

"I deserved it. If someone dropped in front of my feet, I'd probably bop him, too. You've got a powerful swing."

"I was holding back," she bragged. She appeared to go into deep thought for a moment. Then her face exploded with delight. She pointed at a picnic table just outside The Bridge. "So what do you say, Boom Boom? Do you think you're good enough? You want to put it to the test?"

"Good enough for what?" I said in bewilderment.

"Arm wrestling," she said. "Do you want to arm wrestle with me? I've wanted to arm wrestle with you ever since I started hearing the rumors about how strong you are. There's nobody my age who can beat me. I've racked all the guys in my school. You want to try me? Or do you have some sort of bogus idea that arm wrestling with a girl is a no-no?"

I was beginning to admire her personality as much as her looks. "You're on," I said. This was a chance for me to impress her with the fact that the rumors of my strength were based on truth.

She whooped with delight and, after she grabbed the newspaper bag, we tromped out of The Bridge to the picnic table. We sat down opposite each other, made evil eyes for a few seconds, and touched right elbows. Then we held left hands across the table. Even though this was official arm-wrestling position number one, I felt strangely embarrassed. Part of my head was thinking, You're holding hands with one of the most beautiful girls in the world.

Don't be stupid, I argued in my mind. This has nothing to do with holding hands. I'm in a war here. I'm about to do combat.

We grasped right hands.

"You ready, Dog Tweep?" she asked.

I was definitely impressed by her friendly, outgoing personality. "I'm ready, Pond Breath," I replied.

She grinned at me, then squashed her features into a get-out-of-my-face look and counted down. "Three. Two. . . . "

This is going to be so easy, I thought to myself.

"One!"

My biceps and triceps flexed, rippling with power, turning my arm into a powerful lever, poised to drive the back of her hand against the wooden table top. I put all my strength into a crushing wrench, figuring it would be merciful to finish her off fast.

To my surprise, nothing happened.

Gusty's arm and mine remained in the middle of the table, straight up like a tiny CN Tower. I was pushing with all my might and her hand wasn't moving. At all. Unbelievably, Gusty was pushing back with equal force. Her face was red and her eyes were narrowed in concentration, but she was holding me back.

"How are you doing that?" I whispered through my teeth.

"Prepare to die, Little Wimpy Person," she whispered back, taunting me.

Our right hands began to shake. Just a little at first. Then a bit faster. Faster still. Soon our hands were vibrating like a two-fisted tuning fork.

Gusty closed her eyes, and I felt the slight increase in her strength. It wasn't much, but it was enough. My right hand edged down slightly. Lower. Even lower. I tried to find something extra, some reserve of strength to force back her attack. Instead my muscles turned from granite into Silly Putty. They began to burn like I had chili powder for blood. My right knuckles bashed savagely against the wood.

Gusty let go of my hand and flexed her fingers. "Don't feel too bad," she chuckled. "Just feel bad."

I rubbed my arm. "That was amazing."

She waved off my praise. "Naw, in a way, it wasn't fair. I practice all the time with my brothers. They're both in high school. Arm wrestling is a big thing in my family. You should see our table at Christmas dinner when all our aunts and uncles and cousins get together. We arm wrestle between the turkey and cranberry sauce and stuff. My grandma is the best. Even my dad can't beat her and he's big."

I rubbed my arm. "Incredible," I said. "You're good-looking and stronger than me. I never thought I'd ever meet a girl like you. I didn't think girls came like you."

"What did you say? Did you just call me good-looking?"

I nodded, feeling embarrassed for the second time. Maybe she had a thing about people complimenting her looks. I got ready to defend myself in case she reached for another newspaper.

"You don't think I'm too big?" Gusty asked.

"Hey, big is beautiful," I explained.

"You don't think my hair looks stupid? My mom wants me to get it cut. I like it this way. Kind of makes me look like I've been living in the forest with a pack of wolves."

We laughed.

"It's a great image," I agreed.

"You're not just saying nice things because you're afraid I'll use your head for a bowling ball if you say it looks dumb?"

I shook my head. "Think about that. I'm not afraid of anybody."

"I like you, Boom Boom. You want to hang out together?" Then she blushed a little. It was a really cute thing to see. It made her even more perfect. She was sensitive too. "Unless you don't want to hang around with a girl, that is." Her voice dropped down an octave. She sounded almost vulnerable, like she was afraid to hear my answer.

"Hanging out with you would be terrific. What do you do for fun?"

"The usual stuff," she joked. "Chase street cars. Bite a few pit bulls. Eat stuff that isn't food."

We laughed again.

Not only was she good-looking, strong and sensitive, she also had a wonderful sense of humor.

"You want to arm wrestle again?" she asked.

"Naw, not until I practice. You only beat me because I wasn't prepared. We'll try it again in a couple of weeks after I train a bit. Then the outcome will be completely different."

"I'm always going to be number one," she bragged.

"Also, I have to go and get changed."

"Why?"

Geez, I'd almost slipped up and told her what I was going to do that evening. If she found out, it would be game over. She'd think I was a real nerd for sure. "I always change my clothes after school," I fibbed. Then to quickly change the subject, "You want to explore the Watson Mansion with me tomorrow night?"

"How?" she puzzled. "Nobody has been in that place for years. My mom says it's been fenced off since before I was born."

"A buddy of mine says he knows a way in."

"Really? I'd love to do that," she said.

Add brave to her list of good points, I thought.

She punched me in the arm. It was a friendly gesture, a me-and-you-are-good-buddies salute, but it sent a nail of pain into my tricep. Which made me smile. We were perfect for each other.

Chapter 5

The Art Gallery

As I walked up the front steps of the West York Art Gallery, I yanked on the knot of my tie, trying to loosen it. I'd already yanked it thirty times or so on the subway, but I still felt like I was choking.

On my eleventh birthday, my grandmother had given me a lifetime membership to the West York Art Gallery. At first I thought, You've got to be kidding. Me, Boom Boom Bortorowski, go to an art gallery? What is this, a joke? Like I'm going to look at dumb paintings? You've blown a baffle, Grandma.

But my grandmother said, "When you see how truly beautiful some of the pieces of art are, it'll be hard for you to stay away."

To my incredible amazement, she was absolutely right.

On my first visit, I was hooked. And the more I learned about the history of paintings and sculpture, the more I got turned on.

I didn't mind if it rained on weekends any more. I'd head straight to the gallery and spend hours staring at the old Breughels and Rubens.

I especially liked it when they had an exhibit of artwork from someplace else. Like tonight. The opening night of any special exhibition was reserved for members only. I had to wear a tie, but I put up with it because it was kind of neat to hang around with all the people decked out in expensive clothes.

I read the sign on the door: Special Exhibition of Southern Pacific Island Sculpture. Tonight, Art Gallery Members Only.

There was a part of me that wished I could confess my secret love of art to JB and Soso and everybody else. Even Gusty. But I realized there was no way I could explain it to them so they'd understand. Liking old paintings may be okay for other people. People not as tough as me. But it's a definite no-no if your nickname is Boom Boom.

When I entered the lobby, I was greeted by a stern-looking, bearded security guard named Axel. Axel had been working at the art gallery for as long as I could remember. He never seemed too happy about his job.

I liked Axel, even if he wasn't friendly, because he was so big and mean-looking. I had no trouble picturing him eating raw meat on toast for breakfast. I hoped I'd grow up to look like him.

"Welcome," Axel said. He didn't smile. His face stayed frozen in a concerned frown, his voice was deep and low. It rumbled off the marble walls.

I pulled out my membership card and handed it to him, just like I did every time he was on door duty. I figured Axel must not have the greatest memory since he always wanted to see my lifetime pass. Then again, maybe he was just really into his job.

Axel the guard studied it, nodded his head curtly and returned the card. "Please take the elevator to the third floor. The Pacific carvings are in the Blue Room." It sounded more like an order than a request.

The elevator deposited me in a large room full of people dressed in tuxedo-type suits and fancy dresses.

"Ah," I said to myself, "I love this place."

I could see the special carvings arranged on the display shelves on the far wall. They could wait a minute. First, I had to scarf a few of the little meatball things they always had on members-only nights. I headed for the food tables.

I had a mouth full of meatballs and was washing them down with a mug of punch when a girl my age, dressed in a flowered sari-looking outfit, appeared in front of me. She was cute. Not as cute as Gusty, of course. I'd already come to the conclusion that nobody could be that pretty. But she was cute in her own way, even if she wasn't big. Her long brown hair and pale chocolate skin were definitely nice. If I hadn't already met Gusty, and this girl went to school at JAWS, then maybe . . . who knows?

"My name Sonea," she said in broken English.

"Bryan," I mumbled as I swallowed the food.

"Hello, Diane," Sonea said.

"Bryan," I corrected. "Not Diane."

"Biann?"

"You'll have to forgive my daughter." A woman dressed like Sonea appeared behind her. "She is just learning English. Sonea finds it very difficult to pronounce many English words, although she understands what you say fairly well. We are from the island of Loranu. It is north of New Zealand. Have you ever heard of it?"

"No," I answered, wondering if I should have said yes. Wasn't it kind of an insult to say you'd never heard of a person's country?

Sonea's mother didn't seem upset. "We are very small. I am an artist in my country. Some of my carvings are on loan to this art gallery. My daughter is an artist too. She also has a few items on display."

"I'm impressed. I'm useless in art class. Except when we paste the macaroni pieces on the poster board. But even then, I sometimes eat them first." I chuckled to myself. "You ever try that?"

Mother and daughter shook their heads in unison.

"I'm looking forward to seeing your carvings. And may I say how good your English is?" I said to the woman.

Sonea's mother beamed. "Thank you very much. I have studied very hard." With that, she twirled away and began talking to a couple of other members.

"I happy meet you, Bianne," Sonea said.

"My name isn't Bianne. My name is Bryan, but all my friends call me Boom Boom."

"They call you Bum Bum?"

I shook my head. "No, Boom Boom."

"Bum Bum," she repeated.

"Uh-uh. Not Bum. Boom. Boom Boom."

I wondered if it was right for me to be correcting her. Maybe it wasn't polite in her country. What the heck? She couldn't go around calling someone a bum.

"You don't call somebody a bum," I tried to explain. "That's a person who doesn't have a job and doesn't want one, or it's — a bum is where you sit down." I patted my backside. Then I wondered if patting your rear end was a rude thing to do in Loranu. Sonea didn't seem embarrassed. "I'm a Boom. My friends call me Boom Boom."

Sonea pointed at me and said, "Boom Boom." Then she patted her own backside. "A bum bum."

"Right."

"Would you like, er . . . ?" She appeared deep in thought. "Would you like my friend be?"

"Sure," I agreed. "You can't have too many friends. We could be penpals or something."

"My mother think, er . . . send me school in Toronto. A pirate school. Do I say right?"

"Yeah. I think I understand. You're going to come to Toronto and go to a private school. That would be great. If you ever do that, give me a call. I'll show you around the city."

"Tank you. Would you like to see my Undees, Boom Boom?"

"Huh? What? Your undies?"

She nodded her head quickly. "Yes. My Undees. See my Undees. I think they are . . . how I say . . . I think I have pretty Undees."

"Uh." Was this how people got to know each other on her island? This was confusing. "It's a . . . well, I don't want to insult you or nothing, but . . . well . . . "

She seemed puzzled by my reaction. "My Undees are over there."

"Your undies are over there? What are they doing over there?" Did I really want to know?

Sonea made her thinking face for the second time. "I like give you one of my Undees."

"You want to give me your . . . ?" I gasped. "I'm not sure I'd know what to do with your . . . your undies."

Her mother stepped up behind Sonea and rested her hands on her daughter's shoulders. She was smiling at me. "I couldn't help overhearing your conversation. Don't look so worried, Bryan. It is not what you think. The word is spelled u-n-d-e-e-s. An Undees is a stone carving of one of our ancient Loranu gods. Sonea is quite skilled at creating them. She will be a great artist one day."

"Oh," I said with relief. "For a moment I thought, you know. I thought . . . " Talk about feeling like a total geek.

"Sonea has brought some of her Undees from Loranu. They are on display on the other side of the room," her mother said. "She will be pleased to show them to you."

So I followed Sonea through the crowd to a shelf on the far side of the room. On the shelf were a half-dozen small stone carvings, the size of ping-pong balls. They were all of fat people with huge guts and frightening faces. "You made all these?" I asked.

Sonea smiled and nodded. "You like?"

"They're really great. They're so detailed. You've got a lot of talent."

She removed one of the carvings from the shelf and handed it to me. "Please take. A gift."

I studied it. Like the others, it was a fat person with an ugly face. This little statue was obviously female because it had a gigantic bosom.

"This Undees is Loranu goddess, Mekep," Sonea explained slowly, searching for the right words. "If you hold, legend says you be talk to . . . how do you say . . . dead men . . . er . . . ?"

"Ghosts?" I guessed.

She grinned. "Yes, you talk ghost."

"So I'm going to see ghosts if I carry this around?"

"It is legend."

"Thanks a lot. But they're on display. I can't just take it."

She scratched her chin. "It is custom my country. We, er . . . must give away one to first friend we make in new house."

"You sure?"

She nodded.

"Wow. Like, I'm honored. Honest. This is great. I'll keep this forever. Nobody gave me their Undees before. Thanks again."

I slipped the statue safely into my pocket. Immediately, I felt upset. She'd just given me a gift and I had nothing to offer her in return. "I don't have anything to give you."

"In Loranu, there is a . . . er, right time for gift," she explained in her slow English. "Maybe other day, Boom Boom."

I smiled. "Okay, maybe if you come to Toronto to go to school."

Then I noticed another Undees. It was in the corner of the room, alone in a glass box, on top of a pedestal. I pointed at it. "Did you do that one too?"

We walked over to the case. "No," she explained. "This one very old."

I peered at the tiny, fat statue. It looked a lot like

the one Sonea had given me, but the stone was all pitted like it had been left out in the rain for a thousand years or so.

"Mekep?" I asked.

Sonea nodded.

"I guess it's worth a lot of bucks, huh?"

"Pardon?"

"Is it worth a lot of money?"

Sonea nodded again. "It treasure of Loranu. How you say? It is price . . . price . . . ?"

"Priceless." I concluded.

"Yes."

"Pretty, isn't it?" Axel, the security guard, was bending over studying the Undees. He wasn't frowning any more. In fact, his face was etched into a happy grin. That was the first time I'd ever seen him smile. Unusual.

"Yeah," I answered. "Sure wish I owned it."

"Sure wish I owned the money it's worth," the guard chuckled in his low rumbly voice. "So do a lot of other people, I guess. But nobody is going to get this baby. This glass case is attached to a secret alarm only two of us know how to turn off."

"Good," I said, wondering why he'd suddenly become so friendly.

• • •

Sonea and I hung around together for the next hour, checking out the carvings and making fun of some of the stuffy people. Then we were all ushered into an auditorium on the second floor and shown a film about Fiji and the Cook Islands and Loranu and some of the other islands taking part in the exhibition. Loranu looked like a terrific place. Palm trees. Pacific beaches. Tourists in bikinis. I wondered what Gusty would look like in a skimpy bathing suit. What a sight for sore eyes that would be.

I was disappointed when it was finally time to leave. "All good things have to end," I said to Sonea.

She reached over and gave me a gentle kiss on the cheek. I felt myself blush. What a day this had been. I'd met two terrific girls.

"How long you staying in Toronto?" I asked.

She held up her hand. "Days five. On Thor . . . Thorda . . . "

"Thursday," I helped.

"Yes, on that day I am going to ride park with my mother."

"Ride park?"

She made a swooshing sound. "Rolling coaster. I never on rolling coaster."

"You must be going to Wonder World," I said. "That's one of my favorite places. Say, Thursday is a PD day for me. That's when the teachers go someplace and we get a day off. Why don't I meet you at Wonder World and we can go on the roller, sorry, the rolling coaster together?"

Her face lit up. "That be nice. Very nice."

“There’s a big fountain by the entrance. I’ll meet you there at one.”

“At one.”

“Right. See you then.”

“See me then.”

I thought briefly how Gusty would react if she found out I was going to spend a day with another girl. After all, Gusty and I had agreed we were going to hang out together.

I rationalized it by thinking that Sonea wasn’t really another girl. She wasn’t from the neighborhood. She wasn’t even from the country. And West York School didn’t have a PD on Thursday. Just JAWS. What was I supposed to do all day? I’d take Sonea to Wonder World. She’d fly back to Loranu. No problem. What Gusty didn’t know wouldn’t hurt her.

Suddenly, the bearded security guard was standing beside us again. “Excuse me,” he said to me. “I was just admiring the carvings earlier. I noticed the young girl gave one to you.”

“It’s a gift,” I said defensively, thinking that he figured I was trying to steal it.

His laughter rumbled out. “Of course. I merely wanted to show it to Juanita.”

I noticed Juanita, a female security guard, standing behind him. Juanita had only been at the gallery for a couple of months. It was my opinion that she was too short to be a serious threat as a guard. I figured guards should be more like Axel.

"I think all the carvings are wonderful," Juanita declared. "Axel told me about the one you have. I'd really appreciate a close look at it. See how it compares to the others. Would you mind?"

"I guess not."

I dug into my pocket and handed it to her. She turned around for a moment so she could see it in a better light.

"It really is beautiful," Juanita said as she dropped the Undees of Mekep into my hand. "You're an excellent artist," she said to Sonea.

"Thanks very much," Axel added.

• • •

Sonea's mother and the other artists said good-bye to the members as they were leaving the Art Gallery. Sonea walked me to the front door.

"Thanks for a great evening," I said to Sonea's mother. "It was terrific meeting your daughter. I'm going to join you at Wonder World on Wednesday if you don't mind."

"That would be most fine."

Sonea and I shook hands and said good-bye. "I still feel bad I don't have a gift to give you," I said.

"Do worry not," Sonea instructed. "Remember there right time. Maybe you gift to me soon."

"Okay."

I left the gallery and, feeling the best I'd felt in weeks, I started to jog up the street toward the subway stop. I'd only gone half a block when I heard a deep voice calling, "Wait up!"

I twisted around and saw Axel, the art gallery security guard, jogging after me. At the same time I heard another voice say, "Good evening, Boom Boom."

The second voice belonged to Officer Naliwal, one of the half-dozen beat cops who walk the West York neighborhood. Naliwal was also the liaison cop who did the safety lecture stuff at JAWS. He went out of his way to get to know the kids in the neighborhood.

I smiled at Naliwal. At the same time, the security guard dropped from a jog into a walk and, for a moment, seemed reluctant to come any closer. Finally, he walked up to us.

"Sorry to bother you," the guard said to me. "But somebody left a leather jacket back at the gallery. I wondered if it belonged to you."

I shook my head. "It's not mine."

"Oh, all right." He looked at Officer Naliwal for a moment. "Just trying to do a good deed. Nice night tonight, isn't it?"

"Yes, it is," Naliwal agreed.

The cop and rent-a-cop said good-bye to each other by tipping their hats.

"The art gallery?" Officer Naliwal mused. "The art gallery. Now what would Boom Boom Bortorowski be doing in the West York Art Gallery?"

"I know somebody there," I answered. "A girl."

That wasn't a lie.

He grinned. "A girl? I see. That would explain it."

Chapter 6

Access Denied

As I was walking to JAWS down Watson Street the next morning, JB and Erin crossed the street to join me.

"Hey, Boom Boom."

JB threw his arm around my shoulder. "I saw Officer Naliwal outside the wave pool last night. He said he saw you at the art gallery. The art gallery? You? He said you were there with a girl. What's all that about? Do you have a romantic secret?"

"Was it you-know-who?" Erin wondered.

Even the police can have big mouths, I thought. "No, it wasn't you-know-who," I said to Erin. "It was a . . . a friend. A friend of my family."

Then I told them the truth about Sonea and her mom being artists from Loranu. I didn't mention that

I'd only just met her last night and I was at the gallery on members-only night.

"So she's not like a girlfriend or anything?" JB probed.

"'Course not. She's just a friend. I wouldn't be caught dead in the art gallery unless I was doing a favor to a friend."

"What kind of artist is she?" Erin asked.

"A good one. She gave me one of her Undees."

Erin made a did-I-hear-what-I-thought-I-heard expression. "She what?"

"She gave me one of her Undees," I repeated. "She had a whole shelf full. There were all kinds of different Undees. She gave one to me."

JB looked just as stunned as Erin. "No!" he said.

I nodded.

"Why would she give you her undies?" Erin wanted to know.

"She didn't give me all her Undees. Just one. And she gave it to me because she likes me. She makes her own."

"She makes her own underwear?" JB gasped.

It was my turn to look shocked. "I wouldn't know about that, would I? She's just a friend."

"I'm confused," Erin admitted.

"I've got her Undees in my pocket," I continued. "Do you want to see?"

They turned to each other and locked eyes. I could almost hear the He's-got-to-be-kidding in their thoughts.

And that made me laugh. I wished I'd had a camera to record the shocked expressions on their faces. Then I realized that I'd probably looked the same way with Sonea the night before.

I quickly explained to JB and Erin about the carving of Mekep, the Loranu goddess. Then I reached into my pocket and showed them my gift.

"Most stimulating," Erin said as she examined my tiny statue. "You sure had me going for a moment."

"Me too," JB agreed after she passed the statue to him. "And this is supposed to make you see ghosts?"

"That's the legend."

"You seen any yet?" Erin asked.

"Sure. There's one standing beside you right now."

She chuckled.

A black Firebird with dark windows cruised past. There were hundreds of cars on Watson Street all the time. What struck me about this one were the wide drag-racing wheels. "Someday I'm going to own a car like that," I said.

JB and Erin didn't share my enthusiasm for fine automobiles. They didn't even look.

"It's neat how this little statue looks so old," JB observed when he handed the Undees back to me.

I checked it out and, sure enough, it appeared weathered. I'd had it on my bed table all night and hadn't noticed. "That's interesting," I said. "I thought it was smoother. This sort of looks like the one in the glass case."

"What?" JB asked.

"Nothing. I guess the Undees looked different last night in the lights of the art gallery. I suppose they use trick lighting to make things look better."

As I returned the small carving to my pocket, Erin glanced around, then leaned close and spoke in a soft voice. "So tell us about the newspaper girl, Boom Boom. Did you spy on her again?"

Immediately, a bud of anger began to germinate in my intestines. Then I thought about Erin's heating vent secret, and the fact that she had already told JB about Gusty. So I leaned toward her and said in my nicest voice, "Maybe I sort of watched her a little last week. But I'm not going to do it any more. I spoke to her." I didn't bother to explain how I'd fallen out of the roof where I was hiding. "Her name is Gusty."

"Gusty?" they chorused.

"Don't laugh or say nothing, or else you'll be wearing your lunch."

JB held up his hands and shook his head. "I don't think it's funny. I think it's a great name, Boom Boom."

Erin mumbled something. I had my suspicions she was trying hard not to laugh.

• • •

After school, fifteen minutes before I got into deep doo-doo, I was busy typing my story, "Giggling Girls

From Outer Space," into a JAWS school computer.

"So what have you decided to do?" the girl with the antennae asked Jason. "Do you want to come to our planet with us or not?"

"I don't think so," Jason replied. "I'm not really ready to be the only boy on your planet. I don't think I like the idea."

"Why not?" the girl with scales instead of skin giggled. "Think of how special you'll be."

"Yeah," Jason agreed. "That would be all right. It's always special to be special."

"Then what's the problem?" the girls giggled together.

"I don't think I could take it," Jason confessed. "Your giggling is driving me nuts! Why don't you stick a pillow in your stupid mouths?"

"You're really funny," they giggled.

"Here." The scaly girl handed Jason a computer disk. "If you ever change your mind, fire this into your computer. It'll tell you how to reach us."

"Very interesting," Ms Chang declared from behind me. Her voice made me jump. What was with her? Why didn't she want to talk to the front of people's heads?

"It really is an interesting fantasy," the computer teacher went on.

"It's not supposed to be interesting," I said. "It's supposed to be funny."

"Careful, Boom Boom," she warned. "Watch the tone of your voice."

Then she called to JB on the other side of the room. When she had JB's attention, she said, "You two are the only ones coming to JAWS Mob today. I have a dentist appointment, so I have to leave now. The janitor will be in to clean the computer room at four-thirty. You may stay until then, if you wish."

She grabbed her purse and coat. "When Mr. O'Keeffe arrives, it's time to go home. Of course, I . . ."

. . . expect perfect behavior as always, I finished in my head as she finished out loud.

"What are you working on?" JB asked when Ms Chang had left.

"A funny space story," I answered. "Say, JB, I just got an idea. Now that there's nobody here, you want to see if we can get into that disk?"

"What disk?" JB puzzled.

"Don't look so innocent," I said. "Her boyfriend's Wonder World disk. I notice it's still on her desk. What would it hurt if we borrowed it again?"

"I don't think so, Boom Boom. Remember, Ms Chang went strange when she found us messing around yesterday. If she found us playing with it today, she'd go berserk."

"Well, Ms Chang isn't going to find out, is she?" I reasoned. "She's going to be at the dentist. There's nobody else here. So who is going to know?"

"We still shouldn't do it. It's wrong."

I laughed. "You sound like my grandmother. It's like I told Ms Chang. What's the big deal? We just want to see if we can break into the disk."

"Break into," JB stressed. "Even you have to admit that doesn't sound legal." I stood up and walked to Ms Chang's desk.

"Wrong words. How about gain access. Sound better?" I picked up the disk and returned to my computer.

"I still don't know," JB hedged.

I sat down again and fired up the Wonder World disk. "Sure you do. You're just as curious. You want to see if we can get into it."

JB didn't protest any more, so I knew I was right. A few seconds later, he was sitting beside me.

`Welcome to Wonder World. Please enter your security code to gain access` appeared and the silver Wonder World symbol materialized on my monitor.

"Now we try to find a code," I said. "Let's experiment. I read a story once where the security codes for a computer were the names of the planets."

I started with `Mercury.`

`Invalid code. Access denied.`

I typed `Venus.`

`Invalid code. Access denied.`

`Earth.`

`Invalid code. Access denied` seven more times.

"How about names of dances?" JB suggested. "You know, Tango, Foxtrot, Waltz, stuff like that."

We exhausted all the names we knew.

`Invalid code. Access denied.` Every time.

"Fruits," JB said.

I keyed in `Orange.`

`Invalid code. Access denied.`

`Apple.`

`Invalid code. Access denied.`

`Peach.`

`Invalid code. Access denied.`

And so on.

"Let's try body parts," I said.

`Skull.`

`Invalid code. Access denied.`

`Head.`

`Invalid code. Access denied.`

We kept moving down the body.

`Invalid code. Access denied.` Over and over.

Finally I typed in `Toenails.`

`Invalid code. Access denied.`

"You didn't try them all," JB pointed out. "You didn't try . . . you know, private parts."

"Don't be stupid. People wouldn't use a code word

that was the name of your . . . you know."

"Why not? Try it anyway," he urged. "And then try the names of a girl's."

"I hope the janitor doesn't come in and find us typing in these words," I said. "He'll think we're a couple of sickos."

`Invalid code. Access denied.` To everything.

"Now I'm getting upset," I said.

"Whatever you do, don't take it out on the computer. Or me. Maybe you should go outside and punch a tree."

I ignored him. "Maybe we're being too simple. Maybe it's more complicated. What if it's two words? Or more? It could be something like Blue Monday or Hot Chili."

I tried those two suggestions.

`Invalid code. Access denied.`

"Wait a sec. What was that word written on the disk?" I said. "Maybe Raymond Trout wrote the code word on his disk."

"That would be kind of silly," JB noted.

"But people do it," I explained. "I once read that lots of people write their secret code numbers on their bank cards."

I ejected the disk and reread the label. Raymond Trout, Wonder World Computer Technician. Tenderlo . . . Then the big smudge.

I rebooted the disk.

"Tenderlo? That could be it."

So I tried it. `Tenderlo.`

`Invalid code. Access denied.`

I thwacked the top of the monitor with my palm.

"Maybe Tenderlo is only part of it," JB said. "I mean, the label is smudged. Maybe some of the letters have been wiped out."

My snarl turned into a grin. "Smart thinking, JB." I closed my eyes and concentrated. "Tenderlo? Tenderlo? What word starts with Tenderlo? I've got it!"

I typed `Tenderloin` into the computer. "Filet mignon," I said to my friend. "You know, that tender meat."

`Invalid code. Access denied.`

"It could be Tenderfo," JB said. "It could be an F instead of an L. Maybe the word is Tenderfoot."

I was sure it was Tenderlo but I tried Tenderfoot.

`Invalid code. Access denied.`

"Maybe Tenderlo is more than one word," I said. "Tender lo? Tender lost? Tender loud? Tender . . . ?"

"Tender love," JB interrupted.

I keyed `Tender Love.`

`Invalid code. Access denied.`

Then I tried `Tender Loving Care.`

I knew I'd found the right password the minute I attacked the keys. I felt the electronic door open. The screen changed. The silver star and message vanished and white letters scrolled across the monitor.

Hello, Raymond Trout. Welcome to the Inner Sanctum. Press Return to continue.

"What's a sanctum?" JB asked.

"I don't know. Isn't it some kind of special room, like in a church? If we were on the Wonder World computer, we'd be able to access their hard drive. Neat, huh? I wonder what we could do."

I pressed Return and a set of options appeared: Admission, Concessions, Maintenance, Ride Pricing, Ride Status, Souvenirs . . . and so on.

"The dentist was called to the hospital for an emergency," Ms Chang announced from behind us. "So I thought I'd come back to school and . . . what . . . what on Earth . . . I don't believe it!"

I didn't believe it either. Why did Ms Chang insist on sneaking up like that? The anger bubbled and boiled from the deepest part of my gut. It rose up through my stomach and surged up my neck. I knew I was in trouble for having her boyfriend's disk in my computer and that it was my own stupid fault. There was no way I was going to be able to talk myself out of this one. Part of me was ashamed for doing what I did, and for doing it behind Ms Chang's back. It was a pretty scummy thing to do. The feeling of shame only fueled my temper. Then I pictured Ms Chang lecturing me and sending me to the assistant principal's office.

I had no problem imagining Mrs. Bush on the other side of her desk, shaking her head and muttering about what a blob of slime I was and how I wouldn't be allowed in JAWS Mob any more.

I pushed away from the computer desk so hard that it screeched across the floor. The chair toppled behind me.

"Don't say anything!" I shouted at the teacher. "I know I'm in major heck, but I don't want to hear about it."

"Stop shouting this instant!" Ms Chang shouted back.

"Maybe you should cool it, Boom Boom," JB suggested timidly. He looked embarrassed, as if my outburst was somehow his fault.

"Butt out, JB!" I continued to yell. "You know what, Ms Chang? What really bugs me about this is that nobody got hurt."

"I will not tolerate —"

"Leave me alone!" I stomped out the room, kicking the trashcan over for effect. "Leave me alone!"

All in all, a wonderfully mature way to behave. I'd started out neck deep in trouble. Now I was way over my head.

Chapter 7

Follow Me

At seven o'clock, Gusty met me at The Bridge. I was sitting on one side of our arm wrestling picnic table with my head buried in my hands, bemoaning my fate.

"You okay?" Gusty asked.

"Picture your worst day." I looked up at her. "Then multiply it by your second worst day."

"So it's true, huh?" she exclaimed. "The news that's going around the neighborhood is true. I didn't believe it when I heard it."

That made me curious. "What did you hear?"

"I was told that you got mad at a teacher at your school today. You got so mad you chucked a trashcan out a window. Out a closed window."

"What? Who said that?"

"My little brother. He heard it from a friend who's friends with a guy from JAWS whose little brother's in the same Cub pack as him."

"And you believe it?"

Gusty slid into the opposite bench. "My brother doesn't lie. His friend told him you pitched a computer onto the floor and kicked the monitor to pieces. And all the time you were screaming at the teacher to leave you alone."

I brushed my eyebrows with a thumb and forefinger. "It was nothing like that. I hate getting blamed for stuff that didn't happen. What really happened was . . . " I told her the truth about my behavior in JAWS Mob.

"Oh," she said when I was finished. "That's a lot different. I guess things get exaggerated as they pass from person to person. Still, you don't deserve the Mr. Congeniality award, do you?"

"Do you think it was really bad?" I asked. "Was I wrong?"

"Of course you were," she answered quickly. "There was no way you should have been messing around with that guy's disk."

"Okay, maybe using the disk wasn't right. But was I wrong for losing my temper like that? I mean, Ms Chang shouldn't have snuck up on me, right? So it's half her fault, isn't it?"

"Get serious, Boom Boom. You were a moron. An idiot. You were a complete — "

"Thanks," I stopped her. "I'm starting to get the message."

Usually, someone calling me those names would have been enough to make the firecrackers blow up in my head. But Gusty's comments just made me feel more rotten because I agreed with her.

"I love JAWS Mob. Now I'll get booted out of the writing club for sure."

"Did this Ms Chang say that?" Gusty wanted to know.

"She didn't have to. If she doesn't do it, the assistant principal will. Mrs. Bush told me I had to control my temper, or else. Why does stuff like this have to happen to me?"

"Don't whine," Gusty said. "I hate people who whine."

"I wasn't whining."

"Yes, you were. And it doesn't suit you, Boom Boom."

I thought about it. She was right about that comment, too. So I got upset and slowly pounded my fists on the table top.

"You want some advice?" Gusty asked.

I continued to pound. "I'm so mad at myself."

"When you stop bruising the wood, I'll tell you something that might help."

I stopped. "What?" I challenged. "What can I do?"

"It's time for some damage control. The first thing you have to do is accept how stupid you were. Don't get mad about it. Don't whine. Accept it."

"How is that going to help me stay in JAWS Mob?" I asked.

"To tell you the truth, getting kicked out of a writing club doesn't sound all that terrible." Then she quickly added. "But I understand it's a big whoopee for you. Damage control means you try to stop that from happening."

"And how do I do that?"

She shrugged. "I don't know. I don't know because I don't know your assistant principal or Ms Chang. You're going to have to figure out a way to impress them.

"You mean I have to suck up?"

"Nope. They'll spot that. Teachers are real good at knowing when they're being slimed. Whatever you do, it's got to be sincere."

"I guess it can't hurt. I wonder what I can do."

"Something will come to you," she coached. "Give it time. So where's your buddy who knows how to get into the Watson Mansion?"

"Soso should be here any moment," I answered.

As if on cue, Soso Hayes sauntered up to us. "Yo, Boomer," he called. "I knew you'd be here. I knew you'd have the courage to explore the Mansion with me." He patted his backpack. "Got a pair of high power flashlights in here." He stopped and looked at Gusty with a questioning, "Who's this?"

I introduced her. "This is my friend, Gusty Phipps. She's cool."

"Any friend of Boom Boom is a home boy of mine." Soso bowed to her. "Gusty? That's a different name, windy and wild."

"That's me," Gusty stated.

"Did you tell The Gusty One about our forthcoming adventure?" Soso asked me.

"Yeah," I said. "She wants to join us."

"Great. The more the hairier."

"Soso Hayes!" Gusty blurted. "Wait a minute. Now I know who you are. You were caught in the Community Hall thing a couple of weeks ago."

Soso grinned. "And glad to be here today."

• • •

I stared at the Watson Mansion through the three meter high chain link fence that surrounds the entire property. I tried to picture the house a hundred years younger. Maybe it was a pretty building in those days. It certainly wasn't now. It looked like the haunted house in every horror movie ever made — a perfect home for The Addams Family, if they ever needed a new place.

The house was huge, with two pointed towers at each end. The roof was made of red clay shingles. Half of them had fallen loose and lay in shattered heaps on the ground. Some of the planks of the wood siding had warped, and stuck out at strange angles. Several had followed the examples of the shingles and fallen off. I guessed the walls must have been painted brilliant white at one time. Now dirty white paint was peeling off gray wood.

The double front doors were recessed under a curving arch. Over each was nailed a solid sheet of plywood. The windows were shaped like those in an old-fashioned church. They looked like they'd been boarded up by the Mad Carpenter of Watson Street.

Whoever had done the job had hammered the boards haphazardly, as if they were in a hurry to get away from the place.

If the front yard had once been a lawn, you couldn't tell now. It had long ago turned into a mini-jungle of wild grass and poplar shoots.

"*Night of the Living Dead,*" Gusty declared. "That's my favorite old movie. Every time I look at the windows, it always reminds me of the movie. You know, where the people board up the windows to keep the zombies out."

"I know it," I said. "That's my favorite movie too."

We smiled stupidly at each other.

"Maybe there's zombies inside," Soso said.

"I doubt it very much," a voice said with a chuckle. I felt a hand on my shoulder and noticed another hand being placed on Soso's shoulder. "How are we doing, fellows? Gusty?"

I turned to see Officer Naliwal smiling at us.

"You're wondering about this old place, huh?" Officer Naliwal went on. "I wonder about it every time I walk by. I heard that when the Watson family moved out in the seventies, they just boarded up the place and left. One day, the Watsons were there, the next day they were gone. The day they left, this fence was built around it."

"Nobody knows what happened to the Watsons?" Gusty asked.

"We do know who owns the property," Officer Naliwal answered. "One of John Allen Watson's great-granddaughters. She's almost a hundred years old and lives in Fort Myers Beach in Florida."

"I didn't know that." Soso sounded disappointed. "It kind of sounds more eerie to think the family just vanished."

"The land must be worth a fortune," Gusty said.

"I've heard that Malweet's father, Mr. Grewal, offered her a fair price, but she won't sell," Naliwal told us. "She doesn't want to live in it or fix it up, but she doesn't want to sell it either. Most unusual. The Neighborhood Action Committee is apparently going to take her to court to force her to do something. She can't just let the place fall to ruin."

"Yeah, it makes me curious to see what's inside," Soso said. Immediately, he put his hand over his mouth and grimaced. He glanced at me with an apologetic look.

"Me too," Officer Naliwal said. "I'd love to see what's inside that place myself." He removed his hands from our shoulders. "We'll see you around. Take it easy." With that he walked down the sidewalk.

“Sorry,” Soso said when Naliwal was out of hearing range. “I nearly blew it.”

I was distracted by the black Firebird cruising by again. What an awesome looking machine, I thought.

“This way,” Soso said when Naliwal was out of sight.

We followed Soso around the perimeter of the fence to the back. Once upon a time the Mansion must have had a great back yard, sloping down the ravine to Watson Creek. Now it was choked with bushes and unruly weeds.

Gusty grabbed the chain link fence and started shaking it. “So how are we going to get in, Soso? We can’t walk through it. It’s got barbed wire on top, so we can’t climb it.”

“I was exploring here a couple of weeks ago,” Soso explained as he pushed leaves and branches out of our faces. “Right about here, I tripped.” He crouched down and parted some long grass. “I found this.”

We squatted beside him and studied the hole under the fence.

“The rain must have washed it away,” Soso said.

“Or maybe somebody dug it,” Gusty suggested.

“I don’t think so,” I said. “You can see where it’s fallen away.”

“Did you go in, Soso?” Gusty asked.

“Yeah, into the yard. I didn’t go inside the house. But I think I found a way to get in.”

“Show us,” Gusty demanded. She slapped me on

the arm. “This is fun, huh, Boom Boom?”

“Better than eating stuff that isn’t food,” I answered. “Better than chasing pit bulls.”

“Follow me,” Soso said.

Chapter 8

The Watson Mansion

Soso squeezed through the hole like he was a human gopher. He was inside the fence in a couple of seconds. I guess sometimes it's better to be skinny like Soso, because it wasn't so easy for Gusty and me. She succeeded after a few grunts and groans. It took me even longer because I snagged my jacket on a root and had to twist and turn to free myself. Not an easy thing to do.

I lifted myself off the ground and stood beside my friends. For a little while, we didn't say anything. We stood like refugees in a foreign country, staring up at the looming gray monolith we knew as the Watson Mansion.

A little shiver of electricity danced along my spine. This was ultimately exciting. I'm inside the fence, I thought. What made it so incredible was the fact that I passed the Watson Mansion every time I walked to and from school. I did the math in my head. Eight school years times two hundred school days a year times twice a day meant I'd passed that old house over 3,000 times. Add another 1,000 for the times I'd passed it going to the store or the streetcar stop.

The old building had always been there, unchanging, as much a part of the West York neighborhood as The Bridge, a permanent part of the scenery. It was like the pyramids, something from the distant past that would always be around. And I'd always thought of it as something untouchable. I never thought I'd actually get a chance to be inside that high fence.

Now I was.

"What's the matter, Boom Boom?" Gusty asked. "You look like you're on another planet."

"I'm okay. I was just thinking how awesome this is. It's like we're making history. I wonder what JB will say when I tell him? He'll think I'm making it up."

"This way, *mes amis*," Soso instructed.

The sun clung to the horizon, casting mosaic shadows through the tree trunks on the other side of Watson Creek. As it slowly dropped, the air got colder, and I shivered.

"You okay?" Gusty asked.

"Yeah. It's just so cool, all of a sudden."

"I don't notice it," she said matter-of-factly.

We threaded our way through a back yard overgrown with twitchgrass, thistles and poplars. At one point we passed a green, wooden gazebo with the roof half caved in. I tried to imagine it fifty or sixty years ago, freshly painted, emerald bright, with the Watson family sitting around, drinking tea, and maybe talking about the Depression or the war.

"You got that look again," Gusty noted.

"You ever wonder what you would have been like if you'd been born at a different time?" I asked.

"No," she answered. "Why would I?"

End of that conversation.

When we reached the wall, we began to edge sideways toward the back door. Soso passed the back steps without a glance, but Gusty clambered up and thumped on the plywood boarding. "It's solid," she said. Then she jumped down and headed for the planks covering a downstairs window. She attacked those the same way as the plywood. "Same thing. We'll need a crowbar to get in."

"It won't be that hard. Keep following," Soso ordered.

At the corner of the house, jutting out from the wall, was a sloping door recessed in concrete. It reminded me of the door over the storm cellars you see in old movies like *The Wizard of Oz*.

A heavy, rusty chain, secured by an equally rusty

padlock, was threaded through the handle and bolted to the frame. Gusty grabbed the chain and gave it a hearty yank. It rattled, but the door didn't budge. "We're not going to get in this way either," she said.

"Yes, we are." Soso pointed at the two hinges on the other side of the door. "Take a close look. Notice anything about the hinges on this door?"

"Yeah," I said. "They're as rusty as the chain."

"Nope, my good buddies. Check 'em out. See how each hinge is attached by six screws?"

"Right," I said.

"So what?" Gusty added.

Soso pulled a flathead screwdriver from his back pack. "I just happen to be prepared."

"Get rid of the hinges, Soso," I said.

He did as he was told and removed the screws from the two rusty hinges. I shuffled beside him and tried to help him lift the door. It barely moved. So Gusty joined us. It took a fair amount of muscle power by all three of us to flip it backward over the frame.

"Whew," I complained. "That sucker is heavy."

"For the first time in decades, there's a way into the Watson Mansion." Soso put away the screwdriver and removed the flashlights. He handed one to Gusty and the other to me.

"What about you?" I asked.

He pulled out a tiny penlight. "I'll carry it as our emergency back-up in case something happens to the big ones."

Gusty flicked on the flashlight and the beam revealed cement steps vanishing into darkness. "Where do you think it leads, my pretties?" She did a great imitation of the Wicked Witch of the West.

With that, she disappeared down the stairs, her body quickly swallowed by the darkness. A moment later, the light from the flashlight beam vanished, too.

"I've got the other flashlight, so I'll go first. You protect the rear." I carefully eased down the stairs, waving the flashlight in front of me. With each step down, it got a little colder and a little mustier. The air felt heavy, more than humid, like it was about to start to rain at any moment. When I reached the bottom step, I swept the beam in a wide arc, exploring the new environment.

"We're the first people down here in over twenty years," Soso whispered from behind me. "My parents were teenagers twenty years ago. You know, my mom remembers when *Welcome Back, Kotter* was on for the first time. You ever watch that on channel twenty-nine? I can never figure out half the jokes on that show."

"Who gives a flying Frito? And why are you whispering?" I asked.

"It seems like I should," he answered. "We don't want to wake anything up, do we?"

The light bounced off gray rock and mortar walls and nothing else.

"It's empty," Soso whispered.

"I told you not to whisper!" I snapped.

"There's no echo," Soso said softly. "The place is empty and your voice didn't echo. Let's get out of here, Boom Boom."

"There's no echo because it's so damp. Don't go strange on me."

"Where's the Gusty?"

"Gusty?" I called. "Where are you?"

No answer.

The flashlight beam probed the corners. Nothing but cobwebs and walls.

"Where the heck is she, Boom Boom? She only came down a few seconds before us."

"Gusty!" I shouted. This time her name returned as a muffled echo.

"You don't think something has happened to her?" Soso sounded frightened.

"Like what? There's nothing here."

"Nothing we can see. Nothing of this world."

"Don't be a dip."

I let the flashlight rest on an open doorway at the far end of the basement. The door was almost flush against the wall. Behind it were steps leading up.

"That's got to be the basement stairs," I said. "She must have gone up there."

I crept across the basement, cautious and, to be honest, a little worried. Why hadn't Gusty waited for us?

"I don't like this," Soso said, grabbing hold of the sleeve of my jacket. "There could be something evil down here."

"What are you talking about?"

"I hear that in every horror movie I see, so it must be true."

We got close to the doorway.

"Does the air seem cold to you?" Soso asked. "Do you smell something like a demon all of a sudden?"

"I'm not sure," I answered sarcastically. "Let me think. When was the last time I smelled a demon? Was it last week during the science test? Or was it in the shower this morning? No, I think it was — "

"AAARRRGGGHHH!!!" Gusty jumped out from behind the door, screaming and snarling. The flashlight rested on her chin, making her face a mask of sharp shadows. It was a startling effect.

"Arrgghh!" I yelled.

Soso collapsed on the floor.

Gusty immediately began laughing, exploding into hearty Santa Claus-type ho-hos. "Gotcha." She licked her finger and chalked up a pretend number one in the air.

"Got me? Of all . . . you . . . " I tried to breathe normally. I wished my heart would stop pounding like a short-circuited blender. "I . . . you . . . "

"You should have seen your face, Boom Boom," Gusty said. "Your eyes were as big as soup can lids. I spooked you good."

I managed to suck a deep breath. "You . . . you no-good lizard sniffer."

"Lizard sniffer?" she pondered. "Lizard sniffer? Is that the first lame thing you could think of? Lizard sniffer?"

"I should break the flashlight over your head."

"Yeah, you should. I deserve it. But you won't. We've already been through this. You don't hit girls."

"That was yesterday. Now I don't hit any girls, except you."

"You're bluffing, Boom Boom."

"Why did you do that, Gusty?" Soso moaned at our feet.

I reached down and helped him stand up. He swayed a few times before regaining his balance. "You okay?" I asked. "Did you faint?"

He shook his head. "No, my body wouldn't do what my head wanted. My brain was saying, 'Run like the wind, Soso Baby.' But my legs just gave way. Man, was I ever scared."

"I won't do it again," Gusty promised. "If you guys are ready, let's see what's upstairs."

Soso held up his hands. "Not me, comrades. The Soso-meister has been spooked. I am not afraid to admit that right now, right this very moment in time, I am one frightened dude. I need fresh air. I need to go to the bathroom. See you outside." He made a beeline to the unhinged door. "You can give me the flashlights later."

"You up for it?" Gusty asked me. "Or do you want to join your buddy?"

"'Course I'm up for it," I replied.

"I'm glad I met you yesterday," she said.

"Me too you," I replied awkwardly.

We tried to keep our flashlight beams together as we climbed the stairs. Twinned, the lights were almost as bright as an overhead bulb. Every time we took a step, you could see our footprints in the thin layer of dust.

"That was a rotten thing to do," I said. "If it surprised me, imagine how much it must have scared Soso."

"I feel kind of bad about it," she confessed. "A little."

"Are you really as brave as you act?" I asked.

"I psych myself into it," she said. "My mom once told me, 'If you act the way you feel, then you end up feeling the way you act.' I think it's normal to get uptight going into a dark, spooky place. But I don't act it and, all of a sudden, I'm not scared."

A closed wooden door greeted us at the top step. Gusty rubbed her hands across it, brushing a shower of peeling paint flakes into the air.

"Is it locked?" I asked.

"There's only one way to find out." Gusty grabbed the handle, twisted it and flung it open.

Chapter 9

Ghosts?

"Wow," Gusty said. "I don't believe it."

"Incredible," I agreed. "I never thought it would be like this."

The flashlight beams illuminated a huge foyer, three storeys high. What amazed us was that, unlike the basement, the entrance hall was furnished. Some kind of fancy rug hung on one wall. A pair of love seats lined the other wall. They reminded me of the one my grandmother keeps covered in plastic in her living room, the one she brags about being "antique French Provincial." In between the love seats was a small table supporting an ornate vase full of dried flowers. By the doorway was a big wooden coat rack. Heavy winter coats hung on several of the hangers. Next to the coat rack was an elephant's foot umbrella stand, complete with three umbrellas.

"You think that's a real foot?" Gusty asked.

"Yeah," I answered. "Those things used to be in style once upon a time. They still kill elephants for their tusks."

"Some people are so stupid," she complained.

"It's like the Watsons are still living here," I noted. "It's like Naliwal said. One day the family must have walked away and left everything the way it was. Maybe they thought they were going to come back home any time."

Gusty stepped up to the table and rubbed her finger across the surface. "Well, when they do return, they're going to need a maid. The place is a bit dirty." She blew on her fingers and a small cloud formed in the air. "I figured it would be a lot dustier though. After being empty all these years, you'd think it would be layered in the stuff. My parents go nuts when my bedroom has a week's worth of dust."

"Where would the dust come from? The house has been boarded up. I once read that most household dust is made up of the dead skin that falls off the people living in the house."

"No kidding? You mean the stuff I see floating around in the sunlight used to be part of my brother? Gross me out." She touched one of the flowers in the vase. It disintegrated between her fingers. "Twenty-five-year-old flowers. Creepy when you think about it, huh?"

"I just got a weird feeling," I confessed.

"What feeling?"

I pushed one hand into my jacket pocket and absently rolled the statue of Mekep between my fingers. "That it's wrong to be here. Like we're trespassing. I expected the house to be all wrecked or full of old junk. Or like the basement, just empty rooms. But with all this furniture, it feels as if we've broken into somebody's house."

"They're lousy housekeepers then," Gusty said. Obviously, she didn't share my misgivings about breaking into the place.

She walked over to the coat rack to examine the coats and I waved my beam toward the twisting stairway. The stairs were covered with thick, dark green carpet. In front of one banister was a suit of armor posed with a down-turned sword in its right hand. On the other side was a knick-knack cabinet, full of figurines. I swung the flashlight up the steps. As the beam swept across the landing, I thought I saw someone standing in the corner.

The person wasn't in the direct light, so I couldn't see clearly. But standing next to a grandfather clock, there appeared to be a girl dressed in a white smock, with long, dark hair. Surprised, I did a double-take. When I looked directly at her, she wasn't there.

"I . . . she . . . " I let go of the statue as I explored the landing with my light, shining it into the corners and down the second storey hallway.

Nothing.

I was holding the Undees, I thought. Sonea had told me that, in Loranu legend, holding the statue meant I could get in touch with ghosts.

"Naw," I said out loud. "That's just dumb. Don't be stupid."

"What did you say?" Gusty stepped beside me and shone her light upstairs too.

"I think I saw a girl up there on the landing." I detailed what I'd seen.

Gusty looked at me suspiciously. "Right. You're just trying to spook me. You're just trying to get me back for scaring you in the basement."

"No, I'm serious. I think I saw a girl. She was younger than us. Maybe ten or eleven."

"Wooooo. I'm so scared. Hey, look out, Boom Boom, there's a two-headed monster standing right behind you." She walked over to the stairs and examined the contents of the knick-knack cabinet for a moment. "Wow. My aunt collects figurines. I can tell some of these are Royal Doulton. There's a few thousand bucks in this case." Then she climbed the stairs and checked out the landing. She stood next to the grandfather clock. "There's nothing here. There's no footprints in the dust."

"I'm telling the truth, Gusty," I said as I hopped up the stairs to join her.

"I admire how you can do that with a straight face," she said. "But I'm not going to bite. A young girl ghost? Surely you could have come up with a better one than that. Something like a ghost with its guts hanging out."

I sighed. "What can I say?"

"Nothing. Now I figure this place must have thirty rooms. Let's split up, so we can explore them all. I'll go up to the third floor. You check out this one. Shout if you find anything interesting." She charged up the stairs to the third-floor landing. "Oh no, there's a herd of ghosts with their guts hanging out up here," she called. Her laughter trailed to silence as she walked down the hallway.

For a few moments, I stood on the landing and listened to the occasional creak of Gusty's footsteps above my head. Because of Gusty's casual brush off, I wondered if maybe it was my imagination. The only other explanation was that I'd seen a ghost.

And I didn't believe in ghosts. There just weren't any such things.

"Time to do some more exploring," I said to myself. I turned left and walked down the hall.

I'm not sure if Gusty was right when she said the Watson Mansion had thirty rooms, but she was probably pretty close. The hallway was so long, the flashlight beam barely reached the end wall. There were a least six doorways on each side and I imagined there must be a few more I couldn't see in the faraway blackness.

I twisted the doorknob on the first door. It was

locked. So I tried the door on the opposite side. It opened onto a linen closet full of neatly folded white sheets and stacks of white fluffy towels.

Most bizarre, I thought. Why wouldn't they pack this stuff up when they moved? Why leave it here?

The next room had been a play room. A large wooden doll house stood in the center, with a couple of dolls wearing tight skirts and polka-dotted blouses leaning against it. There was an ancient-looking rocking horse in the corner with roller-skates draped over its neck. In the other corner was a play desk. I blew the dust off its slate top. The alphabet, crudely printed in chalk, was still visible. For some reason, that made the tiny hairs on the back of my neck do a little dance.

The shelves on the walls were covered with more dolls, a dozen Hardy Boys books and an awesome collection of old miniature cars, trucks and military vehicles. I picked up a wicked-looking tank and read Dinky Toys embossed on the metal bottom. I remembered my grandfather telling me he had some of those when he was little. He told me he wished he hadn't thrown them away because they were now worth a fair bit of money. I wondered how much I could get for this little tank if I took it.

"No way," I said out loud, and quickly put it back on the shelf.

The next door opened into a storage room. Odd

pieces of furniture, a desk, a couple of chairs, an end table and a large wardrobe with its door half open were piled along one side of the room. Tugged by my curiosity, I opened the wardrobe door the whole way. A fine haze of dust filled the air as the door swung open. To my disappointment, I discovered the wardrobe was empty.

Resting against the end wall were two metal trunks, side by side. I wondered what they could be hiding. I almost flipped open the latches. Then I thought that opening a trunk was different from opening a closet door. First, I'd felt uncomfortable exploring the house. Then I'd felt uncomfortable because the mansion was in such good shape. There was no way I was going to poke around in somebody's trunk, even if that somebody hadn't been around for a long, long time.

A loud noise made me jump with surprise.

There was a mad scrambling sound in the hallway. Two seconds later, something charged through the open door. It was a blur of violent movement, a vibrating bundle of speeding arms and legs.

The thing smashed into my chest with such savage force that I pitched heavily off the trunk and crashed to the floor. The flashlight was bashed out of my hand and rolled across the floor.

Then the thing fell on top of me.

"Ow!" I yelled.

"Ow!" the thing echoed.

If it could feel pain, I deduced, then it certainly wasn't a ghost.

I didn't appreciate being attacked by a . . . by a whatever it was. I reached out for the shadowy mass and grabbed for its neck.

I slipped my hands around its throat and began to squeeze. "Get off of me or I'll . . . " I warned.

"Boom Boom Man," it croaked. "You're choking me."

"Soso?" I said.

"Yeah," Soso whimpered. "Let go o' my neck."

I let go and pushed him off me. "What's the big idea? What are you doing running around like a madman?" I got up and reached for the flashlight. When I shone it on Soso, he was rubbing his neck, trying to catch his breath.

"You nearly killed me," he whispered as I helped him off the floor of the Watson Mansion for the second time.

"I didn't nearly kill you. I was just letting you know I wasn't happy," I told him. "What's the rush?"

Soso looked frightened, as if he had just remembered why he was running through the house like a rabid wolverine. "Keep your voice down, man." His words were coming out soft, but fast. "We're in trouble. I saw somebody crawling under the fence. A real big guy and a woman."

"Cops?"

"They don't look like police. And they ain't the

Welcome Wagon. I don't know what they want but it might not be healthy for us, so I booted inside to warn you and Gusty. All I had was the penlight." He thrust the tiny light at my face. "It was so dark and I started to panic. Then I saw a faint light up here. So I climbed the stairs and charged toward it and that's why . . . Those people, Boom Boom. We have to do something."

"Yeah," I whispered back. This wasn't good news. Soso could be right. Whoever they were, they might not appreciate us being here. We had to find Gusty and get out of the Mansion. "Thanks for coming to warn us, Soso. That was a brave move. You could have stayed outside and hid."

Soso seemed proud of himself. "It was sort of brave, wasn't it? I'm kind of like a superhero dude." Then he checked out the room. "Where's Gusty?"

"Upstairs. Let's go get her."

We both froze at the same time. There were voices in the hall. Two voices. Anxious and angry voices. One of them was deep and powerful. And somehow familiar.

"They're coming this way!" Soso mouthed the words to me.

I pointed at the wardrobe. "In there," I mouthed back.

Quickly, and as silently as possible, we squeezed into the old wardrobe. As I closed the door, it squeaked slightly. "Please don't hear that," I prayed.

I flicked off the flashlight and Soso and I were

draped in a darkness I could taste. I heard my friend breathing in short shallow breaths, an arm's length from my ear. I tried to control my own breathing, making it slower, so I didn't make any sound at all.

A few seconds passed.

A few more.

Feet thudded into the room.

Chapter 10

The Bad Guys

Soso's breath puffed against my face. Puff. Puff. Puff. To me, his rapid breathing was so noisy it filled the whole universe. But I realized that it would probably be inaudible from the other side of the wardrobe door. If we were lucky, the man and woman Soso had seen entering the house wouldn't know we were there. I wondered who they were and what they were looking for.

"I'm sure I heard something in here, Juanita," a gruff voice announced.

"Check in that cupboard," a female voice ordered.

Juanita? It suddenly clicked. Juanita was the name of the security guard at the art gallery. Now I could place the rougher voice, too. It belonged to Axel, the other security guard. What were they doing here?

The door to the wardrobe jerked open, exposing our hiding place. A disposable lighter, held in Axel's hand, revealed the whole awful scene.

"Oh, no," Soso whimpered. "We're dead."

For the first time in my entire life I understood how other kids must feel when they see me walking down the street. I understood why they were afraid. I was face to face with two snarling guards. They were dressed in sweatshirts and jeans instead of their uniforms, but they still looked exceedingly threatening.

Their eyes were wide and white, and Axel's teeth framed by his beard made him look like a shark about to attack. Juanita may have been half Axel's size, but she seemed to grow huge when she lifted up her sweatshirt slightly so we could see a hunting knife in a black leather sheath attached to her belt. She grabbed the handle and removed the long silver blade.

We gasped.

"We're going to die," Soso muttered nervously. "I'm going to die and I haven't even . . . geez, there's so much I haven't done."

The woman waved the weapon in the air, making a sideways figure eight pattern in front of our faces. She was grinning. And I, Boom Boom Bortorowski, who'd never been afraid of anything in his life before, was frightened.

"Put that thing away," Axel ordered. "I told you

we didn't need that. These are just kids. They're going to give us what we want."

"But — " Juanita began.

"Put it away!" Axel repeated angrily.

She reluctantly slipped the blade back into the sheath. "You'd better be right," she warned her partner.

Just because I couldn't see the knife any more didn't make me feel a whole lot better.

Axel grabbed my jacket and yanked me out of the cupboard. Soso stepped out behind me.

"We've found you," Juanita said as she grabbed my flashlight and switched it on.

Found me? What was going on? Why were they in the Watson Mansion? Why were they after me? What had I done? I'm ashamed to admit that my insides floated in a pool of fear. Axel's ugly, angry face and the sight of the knife had really psyched me out. I wished I could vanish, turn into steam and vaporize into the air. I wanted out of there.

Axel flicked off his lighter and twisted my jacket. "Where's the statue that girl at the art gallery gave to you?"

I opened my mouth but nothing came out. My jacket collar was squeezing my throat so tightly I couldn't talk. Now I knew the misery I'd caused Soso a couple of minutes earlier.

"Please don't kill me," Soso begged. "I'm allergic to being dead. I bleed really easily. I'll bleed all over your clothes."

"Be quiet!" Axel ordered. "We're not going to hurt you if you give us what we want."

"Oh, thank you," Soso said with relief. "Thank you. You won't hurt me. Wonderful. Thank you. My mother will really appreciate the fact that you don't want to wound me in any way. Thank you." A pause. "What do we have to give you? You can have the flashlight. You can even have the little penlight. And I've got a dollar and change in my pocket — "

"Quiet!" Axel shouted.

"Got it." Soso nodded his head quickly. "Be quiet. Shut up. Not a sound. That's me. The quiet one. Just pretend I don't exist. You won't hear any — "

Juanita raised her arm as if she was about to hit him.

Soso continued nodding his head, but he didn't say anything else.

Juanita lowered her hand and patted the knife under her sweatshirt. "We won't hurt you if you give us the Undees right now. Where is it?"

Axel twisted my jacket even tighter to emphasize his point. "Hurry up. Where's the Undees?"

I pointed at my throat to tell him I couldn't breathe, let alone speak. He released the tension a little.

"It's . . . " I tried to make spit. "It's . . . in my . . . jacket pocket."

Axel let go of my collar, reached into my pocket and snatched out the tiny statue of Mekep. He quickly examined it. "It's the original." He grinned. "We're rich, Juanita."

My knees were twitching, threatening to give way. So this was how Soso had felt when Gusty popped out from behind the basement door. Part of me was upset that I was so frightened. "I'm Boom Boom Bortorowski," I said to myself. "I'm not afraid of anything."

"Right," another part of my mind taunted. "That's why you're ready to wet your pants. Some Boom Boom!"

And that made me angrier. Angry at myself for being such a wimp. Angry at the guards for making me feel this way.

Axel's face was now etched with an evil grin. "You're curious, aren't you? You're wondering what we are talking about. Why would this carving make us rich? Why did we chase you into this old house to recover it?"

I was so worried about myself, it hadn't crossed my mind.

"I'll tell you," Axel went on.

"Don't," Juanita ordered. "It's not smart."

"What's the harm?" Axel reasoned. "We'll be long gone before these kids talk to the police. And I want the manager of the art gallery to know it was me. That cheapskate turned me down three times when I asked for a raise. Three times. He told me I had a soft job that wasn't worth more than six-fifty a hour.

Five years at six-fifty an hour. It's an insult. I want him to know how I ripped off this treasure."

"We don't have time for this," Juanita said. "Remember, the girl could also be in this house. She might hear us and go tell the police."

Axel grabbed my jacket again. "Where is the girl?" he demanded.

"She didn't . . . " I swallowed, saliva returning to my mouth. I couldn't let them get Gusty. "She didn't come in with us. She was scared of the dark and went home."

Axel released me and grabbed Soso's shirt. "Is that true?"

"Most definitely." Soso nodded.

Axel pushed Soso against the wardrobe and he waved the Undees in my face. "So you think this is the Mekep that the girl, Sonea, carved? But it isn't — this is the statue from the case. The antique."

That explained why it looked different. Then, like a flashbulb from a cheap camera, my brain lit up. I remembered how Juanita had turned away from me for a moment when she was looking at Sonea's Mekep. She must have switched the statues while her back was turned.

Why hadn't I thought of that when my friends noticed how old-looking Mekep was? Maybe this type of stone wears down fast, I'd thought. How dumb could I get? I gave myself a mental boot to the head for being so stupid.

And that made made me angrier still.

"We used you," Axel said. "When we saw you leaving, Juanita removed the one from the case. Do you remember?"

I nodded.

"We knew it would be discovered missing so we had to get the statue out of the gallery fast," he went on. "That is where you came in. Who would suspect a kid of stealing it?"

"You used me to help you steal." I was a little surprised my words came out frothy and bitter. Then I realized that a lot of my fear had been replaced by my anger.

"I was going to follow you outside," Axel explained. "Grab the statue off you, get in my Firebird and vanish. Great plan, huh? It would have worked fine if you hadn't stopped to talk to the cop."

The Firebird with the darkened windows and racing tires? "You've been following me all day."

"Right," Axel said. "I got your address from the gallery's membership list. I've been cruising around watching you, waiting for the right moment, waiting for you to be someplace out of sight."

"You won't get away with this," Soso said. Like me, he sounded braver than he had a minute ago. "We'll tell the police."

Axel dismissed that threat. "So what? We'll lock you in this room. By the time you escape to inform the cops, we'll be impossible to find."

The ceiling creaked.

We all looked up.

It creaked again. And again.

The guards stared at me for a moment, then eyed each other.

"The girl," Juanita said. "They lied."

Slowly, as if she was enjoying the effect she was having on Soso and me, she unsheathed the knife again and rubbed her thumb lightly along the blade, testing its sharpness. "I'll take care of her."

The anger simmering in my stomach boiled and suddenly shot into my brain. Like a mental kaleidoscope, my thoughts twisted and stretched into a familiar pattern. I got me back. Me, Boom Boom Bortorowski. The toughest and meanest kid at JAWS, the toughest and meanest kid in West York. My courage returned. For the last few minutes, I'd been acting like Super-Wimp. I'd let them threaten me and push me around. But I sure wasn't going to let them threaten Gusty.

No way.

"You guys have made me mad. It's not healthy to make me mad." A growl rolled from my bowels and erupted into the room. "Yaaarrrr!"

Juanita jumped back, completely taken by surprise. Startled, she let the knife fall from her hand. Real fast I kicked at it, sending it across the floor and under the cupboard. They'd have to do some heavy moving to get that weapon back.

"Call me Boom Boom!" I said. I waved my fists in the air and screamed like a toddler having a class ten temper tantrum.

"Holy . . . " I heard Soso mutter from behind me.

"Stop that!" Axel tried to to make his voice stern and authoritative, but I heard the slight waver in it. The fact that I was pulling a hairy conniption fit was distressing him.

What Soso had done to me in the cafeteria line was my inspiration. I lifted my left foot and thudded it back down on the toe of Axel's right shoe. The heel of my Blacktops crushed the leather.

"Ow-woo!" Axel howled.

Considering how small the room was, I did a nifty half-spin and repeated the procedure on Juanita's toes.

"Ouucch!" she yowled.

"Yaaarrrr!" I roared again, then bent over and drove my head into Juanita's gut.

"Oomph," the guard moaned as she collapsed.

When I twisted back to Axel, he was holding his arms across his stomach so I couldn't ram him, too.

"You've made a big mistake, kid. I am going to teach you a lesson. You'll — "

"Yaaarrrr!" I charged at him and smashed his forehead with a perfect head butt.

Therwack!

Axel wore a mask of disbelief for three seconds, then his eyes rolled slowly upward and he collapsed against the trunk. I grabbed the Undees from his hand as he slumped to the floor. Then I retrieved the flashlight from Juanita.

"Wow!" Soso congratulated. "Awesome. Incredible. I wouldn't have believed it if I hadn't seen it. How do you do that without hurting your head?"

"You don't," I told him as I rubbed the helmet of pain surrounding my head. A looney-size bump was growing on my hairline. "Why did I do something so dumb?"

Without the cyclone of anger roaring through my body, I understood just how careless I'd been. I'd attacked two criminals. I glanced at Juanita. She was holding her stomach and groaning, gradually recovering her wind. Axel had regained consciousness and was looking up at me with a glassy, but rapidly clearing, gaze.

"Perhaps this is a good time to make a hasty exit," Soso suggested.

"A real good time," I agreed and slipped the Undees back into my jacket.

We reached the door at the same time and bounded off the doorframe.

"Watch it!"

"Sorry, man," Soso said. "I just want to get out of here."

We scrambled through the door, first Soso and then me, and charged down the hallway. Soso started to run down the stairs but I grabbed his arm to stop him. "First, we get Gusty."

I shouted up the stairway to the third floor. "Gusty!"

"Gusty!" Soso added in a voice twenty decibels louder than mine.

There was no answer. I couldn't see a glow down the third storey hallway. That meant that Gusty had to be inside a room. I wondered if she could hear us.

"Gusty!" Soso yelled again.

"There, Axel! On the landing!"

We swivelled around and saw Juanita standing outside the storage room pointing at us. She was supporting Axel, who was rubbing his head. When Axel focused on us, he quickly regained his senses, formed his face into a vision of insane fury and bolted down the hall toward us.

Soso darted down the stairs, three steps at a time. "Let's get outta here! Let's get Officer Naliwal."

I couldn't leave without Gusty. If I ran away with Soso, one of them might follow me, but the other could scoot upstairs to get Gusty. I couldn't let that happen. But what could I do? There was no way I'd be able to stomp on their feet again. If they caught me, they'd probably . . . I wasn't sure what they'd do, but instinct told me it wasn't going to be a pleasant experience.

A plan flashed into my mind. I moved to the edge of the landing and watched the two guards charging furiously towards me.

"It is useless to run away," Axel shouted. "I will catch you. And when I do . . . "

"Come on," I shouted back. "Come and get me."

When they were three steps away, I switched off the flashlight. The landing was instantly enclosed in a curtain of total blackness. I dropped to the floor and wisely covered my face with my arms. I didn't want a real boot to the head.

My plan hinged on two things. First, I figured that as soon as the light vanished, the guards would try to stop before they hit the stairs. They'd probably be able to do that in three steps. What they wouldn't expect was my sprawled shape waiting for them. They'd pull up short of the top step and then trip over me to fly head first down the stairs. The thick carpet would stop them from being really hurt, but hopefully they'd be so disoriented that I'd be able to get Gusty and get out of the Watson Mansion before they could regroup.

A shoe thumped into my ribs and the sharp pain made me yelp. My cry was drowned out by Juanita's howl as she did a Supergirl impression somewhere in the darkness above my head.

Another foot bumped against my leg. I waited for Axel's cry as he followed his co-conspirator on the express route to the first floor. Unfortunately, I could tell by the shuffling of feet on the carpet that Axel had maintained his balance.

Meanwhile, there was a series of noises as

Juanita flopped down the stairs. *Thadump. Thadomp. Thadump. Crash!* It sounded like someone had wiped out a supermarket aisle of canned goods.

The armor, I thought.

Then there was light again.

Axel was standing above me, his face and the landing eerily lit by the swaying flame of his lighter. "So, you are on the floor, huh? That is good, because that is where you are going to be for a long, long — "

FABUMP!

" . . . timeaaaaaaaaaaaa!" he hollered as he flew over my outstretched body.

The space where Axel had been was immediately filled by the towering shape of Gusty Phipps and her flashlight. She still had her arms out straight.

"I heard lots of noise. When I looked down, it appeared that you needed a little help," she said.

Axel followed Juanita on a wild ride to the first floor. *Thadomp. Thadump. Thadomp.* Crash! The knick-knack case and its contents exploded in a spray of sparkling fragments.

"That's too bad. Those were expensive figurines," Gusty said. She shone her light on the sprawled bodies of the gallery guards. "Do you want to tell me what's going on? Who did I just wipe out?" She rested the beam on Juanita. "I thought you didn't hit girls."

"She's not a girl. She's a thief. And I didn't hit her. I stepped on her foot, head-butted her gut and tripped her. That's not hitting," I said as I jumped to my feet and grabbed Gusty's hand. We imitated Soso, taking the stairs three at a time. I wasn't going to wait around for the Deadly Duo to recover and chase us again. My number one priority was to get safely outside the Watson Mansion.

We hurtled through the empty basement, dashed out the cellar door and flew across the overgrown back yard. We were struggling through the hole under the fence when Soso Hayes and Officer Naliwal ran up to us.

"I've called for a couple of squad cars," Officer Naliwal informed us as he helped me to my feet. "Where are those people?"

"Inside," Gusty answered. "They had a little accident."

"Be careful," I added. "I have a feeling they're not going to be happy to see you." I handed the statue of Mekep to the policeman. "This doesn't belong to me. Believe it or not, it's worth a lot of money."

"Wow," Soso said. "We caught some bad guys. We saved a valuable treasure. We're hero dudes."

Chapter 11

Wonder World

Sonea and I grinned at each other as we waited in line for the Weird Water Roller Coaster in Wonder World. It was the sixth time we'd stood in that line, waiting to squeeze into the tiny two-seat car that thundered through the pools of water at the bottom of every roller coaster hill. Like Soso, I wondered how come the little car didn't fly off the rails.

I'd met Sonea and her mother by the big fountain at one o'clock just the way we'd planned. We'd spent a half hour talking about the adventure in the Watson Mansion and the recovery of the special Mekep.

Then Sonea's mom had suggested, "Perhaps it is better for you two young people to enjoy this day together. I think I will find a place to do some reading. I will meet you back at this fountain at closing time."

It sounded like a fine plan to me.

"You feel sick yet?" I asked Sonea.

"Sick? I not do have cold," she answered.

"Not ill. I mean, you feel like you're going to puke from going on the rides yet?"

"Puke?"

"Upchuck. You know, spew chunks? Hurl your cookies." I made a face like I was feeling nauseous and she giggled.

"I no hurl my cookies," she said.

We were having a terrific time, despite the fact we couldn't talk to each other all that good. Spending the PD day with Sonea was a great move.

Like I'd done every five minutes for the last couple of days, I thought about what had happened in the Watson Mansion. I rubbed the bump on my forehead. It was still tender, but I no longer had a headache. It had gone away yesterday. I wondered how Axel's head felt.

Apparently, the art gallery guards were okay . . . physically. According to Officer Naliwal, they suffered only a few minor cuts and bruises from their wipeouts with the armor and knick-knack case. As for their mental health, they were probably extremely depressed.

"They could spend a few years in jail," Naliwal had said. "They are in serious trouble."

While Sonea was watching the ride, I studied her face. She was definitely cute in an un-Gusty sort of way. "Are you having fun?" I asked.

"Yes. Very yes. It fun be with you."

We heard another siren coming from the far side of the park. It was the third time we'd heard a siren in the last half hour. I wondered if maybe Sonea and I should check it out.

I felt slightly guilty about spending the PD day with Sonea at Wonder World while Gusty was slaving away in school. And I felt bad that Gusty didn't know I was with another girl. But Sonea was flying home to Loranu on the weekend. And, even though her mother had definitely decided to send her to school in Toronto, she wasn't coming back until next year.

Besides, I had bigger things to feel guilty about.

My mother was majorly upset that I went exploring the Watson Mansion.

"It was such a stupid thing to do, Bryan," she lectured when Officer Naliwal took me home. "You could have been hurt. Or worse."

When I think about it, she's right. Gusty and Soso and I could have been in serious trouble. Things could have been more than nasty.

But at the same time, I knew my folks were proud of me for the way I handled the gallery guards. I could tell they were pleased I'd taken care of myself and my friends.

"Just don't ever do it again," Mom had threatened.

"No problemo," I'd promised. "I don't want to feel like that again. Ever."

Also, I felt guilty because the cops were so mad at me.

Oh, they were delighted about recovering the stolen statue, of course. And happy they'd caught the thieves. But they were still angry at my friends and me.

"No matter how you look at it," Officer Naliwal lectured after he'd praised us for recovering the Undees, "you shouldn't have been in the Watson Mansion. Maybe it's not break-and-enter since nobody lives there any more and you didn't plan on taking anything, but it's still trespassing. You were somewhere you were not supposed to be. And property was damaged. We're going to have to inform the owner of this incident. If the owner wants to press trespassing charges against you, there's nothing I can do to stop it."

But some stuff was working out just fine. After my parents reamed me out on Tuesday night, I went to my room and followed Gusty's advice. I tried some damage control. I wrote a letter to Ms Chang.

I apologized for my attitude when she'd found me messing with her boyfriend's disk. I explained how I knew I was wrong and I had no excuse for talking to her the way I did or kicking the garbage can. I promised it wouldn't happen again and she had my promise in writing.

Then I told her I was going to Wonder World on Thursday and I'd personally return the disk to her boyfriend, Raymond Trout, and I'd apologize to him too.

Then I wrote a letter to Mrs. Bush telling her how those few minutes in the Watson Mansion had let me see things real clearly, and I'd definitely reformed this time. She too had my promise in writing.

I slipped the letters into their staff mailboxes before morning announcements on Wednesday. About ten minutes into first period, I was called to the office. Ms Chang and Mrs. Bush were waiting for me in the assistant principal's office.

Ms Chang made a tight little smile when I entered. She was grasping my note in her hand. "Apology accepted," she said. Then she handed me her boyfriend's disk. "I've called Raymond and he'll meet you outside the control building tomorrow at four in the afternoon."

"I'll be there," I promised. "I know where that is."

Then Ms Chang left the office and left me to the mercy of Mrs. Bush.

I studied the diplomas on the walls, the shelves and her messy desk to distract myself. I was worried what my punishment was going to be. I was expecting the guillotine or something equally horrible. Of course, my worst fear was being chucked from JAWS Mob.

"Boom Boom, I read your letter," Mrs. Bush began.

Boom Boom, I thought. She's calling me Boom Boom, instead of Bryan.

"And taking into account the terrifying experience you went through yesterday, I'm going to believe that you are sincere in your desire to reform your behavior this time."

And that was it.

Neither Ms Chang nor Mrs. Bush even threatened to kick me out of the Mob. Thanks to Gusty's good advice.

I checked my watch. It was nearly four. I patted Raymond Trout's disk in my jacket pocket and realized I had to get to the control building which was on the far side of Wonder World.

"I have to go someplace for a couple of minutes," I told Sonea. I checked out the line-up. It would be another minute or two before we got on the ride. The ride itself lasted a few minutes. That should be enough time to see Raymond Trout, hand him his disk, say I'm sorry, and get back as Sonea was getting off. "You go on the Weird Water by yourself this time. I've got something to do. I'll be back in a little while. Will you be okay?"

"Yes. Not as fun without you."

"We'll go on together later. Don't leave here. Wait for me."

"Okay, Boom Boom."

I left the line and jogged toward the control building. I was surprised to find it surrounded by a fire engine, an ambulance and a police car. Two paramedics were wheeling a stretcher out of the door and into the ambulance. My heart stopped for a moment when I saw the person on the stretcher. It was Raymond Trout. With the siren blaring, the ambulance pulled away.

I shoved through the watching crowd and got close to where a fireman was talking to somebody dressed in a Wonder World jacket. I couldn't hear everything they were saying but I understood most of it.

Fire Guy: " . . . carbon monoxide build-up from portable diesel unit . . . vented through control building . . . should have turned off the air conditioning . . . guy just overcome . . . who was he?"

Wonder World Guy: " . . . technician . . . Trout . . . medics say he's going to be okay."

Ms Chang's boyfriend in an accident? At least, he was going to be all right. What a crazy week this was.

I didn't have long to ponder how crazy it was because a police officer ran out of the control building and approached the two men I was standing beside. "We've got a big problem," she said. "We need another computer tech here right away. Is there one on site?"

The Wonder World representative shook his head. "No, Raymond is the only computer technician working this shift. We don't keep full staff on weekdays this late in the season. But I can call somebody. It'll only take a half hour or so."

The cop looked more than worried. "There's no time."

"What's up?" the fireman asked.

She pointed at the Weird Water Ride. "The phone in the control room just rang. When I picked it up, it was the operator of that ride. She said they had a transformer blow and burn out their controls. They managed to stop all the cars except one. Somebody's stuck on it and they can't stop it."

"Can't stop it?" I gasped.

I glanced back at the ride. Even from this far away, I could tell that the person stuck on the ride was Sonea. I could see her Loranu sari, the neck scarf flying out behind her. As the Weird Water Roller Coaster car screamed down the big hill, I could tell it couldn't go any faster without breaking apart. When it hit the pool, it threw up a wall of water. Sonea was bashed viciously against the seat.

I held my breath and remembered Raymond Trout's words to me in the computer room on Monday night. "If that ride goes even ten percent faster than it's supposed to, the little car will smash to pieces when it hits the water pond."

"Oh my," I muttered. "This can't . . . that's my friend on that. You've got to to do something."

They've got to stop that thing before she's killed, I thought.

I was as scared as I'd been when Axel had opened the cupboard. I'd been in trouble then. Sonea was in worse trouble now. Something terrible could have happened to me. Something terrible was going to happen to Sonea.

"Can't the operators do anything?" the Wonder World rep asked.

The police officer shook her head. "They told me they couldn't. They said all their controls were dead. They said they needed a computer override."

"Oh, no," the rep moaned. "There's got to be somebody in the park who knows how to operate that computer. Let me think. I've got to find somebody who knows how to use that computer system in there or . . . " His words trailed off.

"There has to be somebody!" I yelled. "That's my friend!" I felt so frustrated. There had to be somebody.

"Take it easy, son," the cop said. "We'll find a way."

"You're really funny," they giggled.

"Here," the scaly girl handed Jason a computer disk. "If you ever change your mind, fire this into the computer. It'll tell you how to reach us."

My story, "Giggling Girls From Outer Space." Why would I think of my story now?

Computer disk? Reach us?

"Raymond's disk!" I shouted out loud.

Everyone turned around to look at me.

I grabbed the disk from my jacket pocket and waved it in the air. "I can do it."

The cop tried to grab me as I ran into the control building, but I made a nifty head fake and her arms waved harmlessly in midair. I dashed through the door and saw the computer console on the far side of the room. I rushed over, hopped into the chair and slipped in the disk.

Instantly the silver star and `Welcome to Wonder World. Please enter your security code to gain access` flashed on the monitor.

I typed in `Tender Loving Care`. The welcome vanished and `Hello, Raymond Trout. Welcome to the Inner Sanctum. Press Return to continue` appeared in its place.

I heard people behind me. "What can you do, kid?" the Wonder World rep was saying. "What can you do that we can't?"

Chapter 12

Weird Water Roller Coaster

I tapped the Return key and the menu appeared.

"I think I can get the computer to stop the ride," I announced. "I'm not sure, but I saw something while JB and I were messing around on Tuesday. Something I can use."

"What are you talking about?" It was the firefighter speaking.

I accessed the Wonder World file and searched the options list. `Admission, Concessions, Maintenance...`

Then for a moment, I couldn't do anything.

Nothing.

Why was I staring at the monitor and not doing

anything? The problem was, I was scared something was going to happen to Sonea. It was the same as being afraid for myself — and yet it was different. It was slowing me down. I wanted to help her and I didn't want to make a mistake.

I was trying to read the words, but they resembled an alien language. They seemed all jumbled and confused. Why couldn't I find what I was looking for?

...Ride Pricing, Ride Status, Souvenirs...

There it was! That had to be the way in.

Ride Status.

That was the file I'd seen on Tuesday. That's what had triggered the idea in my head.

I keyed Ride Status.

Command not understood. Please re-enter or press the option key to quit program.

Huh? I reread what I'd typed. Ride Atatus.

"Of all the wrong times to make a stupid typo!" I said.

"I'm not sure about this," the Wonder World rep said.

"Let him try," the cop said. "What else can we do?"

I re-keyed Ride Status.

For safety reasons, this file is restricted to technician personnel only. You must have Priority 5 clearance to proceed. Please input your access code to continue.

"What's that mean?" the fireman asked.

I banged my palm against my forehead. "It's not good news. I hope it doesn't mean we're locked out."

What was the chance Raymond Trout would have Priority 5 clearance? You probably had to be an engineer to have that. But I had to try. I keyed `Tender Loving Care.`

`Proceed Raymond Trout. You are accessed into Ride Status. Which ride do you wish to alter?` the monitor asked.

"Yes!" I cried. "All right. Let's hear it for the important Raymond Trout." I let out my breath. But my fingers didn't want to find the right keys. It seemed to take forever to input `Weird Water Roller Coaster.`

I glanced out the open door at the ride.

"Those sparks you see beneath the car are from the asbestos control brackets," the fireman said. "They are burning off. I'm afraid as soon as the car hits the pool on the next circuit, it'll go."

My monitor dissolved into a new set of messed up words. It seemed to take a long, long time before they made any sense to me.

`What do you wish to adjust on the Weird Water Roller Coaster? Please select your option by number.`

`1) Speed`

`2) Interval`

`3) Load capacity`

Why couldn't I read faster?

4) Maintenance

5) Repair Reports

"Try number one," the cop called from behind me.

Speed. I have to slow down the speed.

I keyed 1.

The screen dissolved into gobbledygook for a second and then Sorry, on site problems make it impossible to adjust that function. Do you wish to continue?

I pounded in Y.

Please select another number.

Another number? What would work?

2) Interval.

Interval? What the heck did that mean? I slammed the 2 key.

Sorry, on site problems make it impossible to adjust that function. Do you wish to continue?

"She's climbing the hill," the Wonder World rep said. "She's climbing the hill before the pool."

I glanced and saw her watching Sonea on the ride on a TV monitor. I typed Y.

"I . . . don't . . . know . . . what . . . to . . . do . . . next." My words came out like my thoughts — slow, sluggish, covered in grease.

"Try another number, kid," somebody said.

Please select another number.

I pressed 3.

Sorry, on site problems make it impossible to adjust that function. Do you wish to continue?

Frustrated, I typed 4, expecting the same message to blink on the monitor.

In slow, slow scroll, a new statement appeared on the screen.

Your maintenance request has been noted. Do you wish a complete electrical shutdown of the Weird Water Roller Coaster while maintenance is performed?

"That's it," the cop shouted through the fog. "If you cut off the power, it'll stop the ride. Type in yes. Hurry."

If it's possible to smash something with your index finger, then I smashed that Y key as hard and as mean and as savagely as I could. I tried to drive it through the computer, through the desk and through the floor.

Complete shutdown in effect. All power to the Weird Water Roller Coaster has been disconnected. It is now possible to perform all maintenance chores.

I stood up and charged outside. Everyone followed.

Sonea's car was almost at the top of the hill before the drop toward the pond. I knew by the speed of the car that, if it crested the rise, Sonea wasn't going to make it.

We held a collective breath.

"It's not going to stop," the Wonder World rep whispered.

"No, it's slowing," I said. "The car is slowing down. Look."

"You're right," the cop agreed. "You're right." She sounded like a little kid on Christmas morning.

"It has to stop before it goes over the top," I said.

The was a violent lurch to the car and Sonea was bumped against the restraint and then thrown back into her seat.

"It's stopped!" the Wonder World rep shouted. "And look, she just waved. She's all right."

The firefighter patted my shoulder. "Way to go, good buddy. You did it. You're a hero."

"That was brilliant," the cop said. "If someone had told me at breakfast what I'd witness today, I would have never believed them. What's your name, son?"

All of a sudden, I felt ultra-tired. My shoulders slumped like I was carrying a mega-weight. I smiled at the woman police officer.

"They call me Boom Boom."

Chapter 13

I Know That Girl

The next day, Friday, I ate lunch in Watson Park with JB and Erin. We sat at the picnic table outside The Bridge.

"Been quite the week for you, Boom Boom," JB said as he read a story in the *Toronto Sun* he'd just bought at Yeung's convenience store. "It says here that those two guards are going to plead guilty."

"My dad read it to me at breakfast," I told him. "I don't even want to hear about it any more. Those reporter guys drive you nuts. I wish Mrs. Bush hadn't called the newspapers to tell them what I did."

"I felt the same way after the Community Hall thing," JB confessed. "After a while you get sick of seeing your picture on the TV, right, Erin?"

"I kind of liked it," Erin observed. It was the first

comment she had made. Silence was a strange state for Erin. All lunch she'd had her head buried in her book, *Famous Families of Toronto*. "JB and I are going to get some kind of hero medals from the city. They going to do the same for you?"

"I don't know," I answered. "The president of Wonder World has called a press conference for next Monday. He wants me there. I'm going to meet Raymond Trout and get some kind of reward."

"Maybe it's a free lifetime pass to Wonder World," JB suggested.

"I could handle that," I said.

"Can I ask you something, Boom Boom?" JB said after he finished his juice box. "I've noticed that every so often you've been flexing your arm muscles in class."

"So?"

"So I've noticed that it's just your right arm."

"My arm wrestling arm," I told him. "I'm trying to build it up. I've been lifting my dad's weights every night."

"You planning on entering an arm wrestling contest?" Erin asked.

"Nope, but you can never tell when you're going to get challenged." I peeled the wrapper on my dessert cake and figured I'd be ready for a rematch with Gusty in a week."

"How is Sonea?" Erin wanted to know.

"Great. She called me last night. Did I tell you her

mom is definitely going to let her go to school in Toronto?"

Actually, Sonea had spent most of the phone call praising me in broken English for saving her life. It made me feel embarrassed.

"I told you right time to give gift," she'd said. "You found right time."

"The art gallery may send Soso, Gusty and me on a vacation to Loranu as a way of saying thanks for catching the crooks," I continued.

"Wow!" Erin exclaimed. "I'm jealous. What a chance. When are you going?"

"Not sure. They just said maybe. I hope it's sometime in the middle of winter. Then I'll be thinking of you guys when I'm there. It should be cold and snowy in good old T.O. in January."

"Nice guy," JB grumbled.

"Was Gusty jealous when she found out you went to Wonder World with Sonea?" Erin asked.

"She still doesn't know. She just thinks I saved somebody. Not somebody I knew. So don't tell her."

"What are you going to do when Sonea comes to live here?" Erin wondered. "What are you going to do with two girlfriends?"

"That's next September. I'll worry about it then." I finished my cake and stuffed my garbage into my lunch bag. "There's a Dickee Dee guy over there. Can I treat you guys to a popsicle? Celebrate my good fortune about the Watson Mansion and Wonder World?"

"You're lucky the old lady in Florida who owns the mansion didn't want to charge anybody with trespassing," JB said.

"She just told the police to lock the house back up and send her the bill," I noted. "Strange, huh? You'd think she'd be major fumed. The thief wiped out thousands of dollars worth of figurines. There's a real mystery to that place. I figure I haven't finished with that old house." I handed JB a couple of dollars. "I'm buying, but you're fetching."

"A deal." He jumped up and headed for the Dickee Dee cart.

I focused my attention on Erin's book and felt my stomach drop into my Reeboks.

She looked at me with a puzzled expression on her face. "What's up, Boom Boom?' she said. "You look like you've seen a ghost."

I reached over the table, gently lifted the book from her hands and pointed to one of the photographs. It was a photo of a girl dressed in a white smock. She was wearing black lace-up boots and had shoulder length black hair with eyebrow length bangs. It was the girl I'd seen on the landing in the Watson Mansion. "I know that girl, Erin."

"You can't," she said in a bewildered voice. "That's a picture of Sarah Watson, one of John Allen Watson's granddaughters. It says she died of pneumonia when she was ten years old."

JB plonked back down on the bench with three

orange popsicles. He regarded Erin and me. "What did I miss?"

"I have to get back into the Watson Mansion," I told them.

MARTYN GODFREY moved from England to Canada at the age of eight. He failed grade three, and hated writing because he couldn't spell. Practice paid off, however, and by grade five he was enjoying school, especially creative writing.

Martyn's writing career began when, as a teacher, he was challenged by a frustrated student to write a story. That challenge resulted in the publication of his first novel. He has since written dozens of books and has become one of Canada's most popular authors. Martyn spends his time writing, visiting schools, reading comic books and hanging out with his two kids.